BITTERROOT BADLANDS

STONECROFT SAGA 10

B.N. RUNDELL

WOLFPACK
PUBLISHING
—— EST 2013 ——

WOLFPACK PUBLISHING
— EST 2013 —

Bitterroot Badlands

Paperback Edition
Copyright © 2020 B.N. Rundell

Wolfpack Publishing
6032 Wheat Penny Avenue
Las Vegas, NV 89122

wolfpackpublishing.com

Paperback ISBN 978-1-64734-982-0
eBook ISBN 978-1-64734-981-3

BITTERROOT BADLANDS

DEDICATION

To my muse . . .
. . . my sweetheart,
. . . my lover,
. . . my best friend,
. . . my partner for life and eternity!

1 / GREENUP

He could smell it. The breeze from the high mountains that whispered down the valley carried the freshness of spring that breathed life into the wilderness. The aspen were showing their red buds that would soon burst into the bright green of the quakies that shone like crystalline emeralds that lay in the folds of the black timbered mountains. The conifers were pushing forth their new needles and cones, the biting newness refreshing the decay of the forest floor. The window of the cabin had been thrown open to air out the stuffiness of the long winter and the men had been sent to the lake to scrub off the stench of the unwashed. Gabe paused at that point on the trail that overlooked the valley below the cabin, lifted his head high, took a lung filling breath and smiled, "Yup! I now pronounce it to be officially springtime!"

A low rumbling chuckle came from his life-long

friend, Ezra, "And just who appointed you the lepre-chaun of the lake?" Ezra was the more solidly built of the two, broad shoulders over a massive deep chest and bulging arms, his black beard, a token of the long winter, framed his burnt brown face and black pools for eyes, but an unmistakable mischievousness and deep wisdom shown from his ever-present smile. Often referring to himself as black Irish, he was the son of the pastor of the largest colored church in Philadelphia and a mother that was truly black Irish from the old country. Like his mother, he was gifted with the ways of the ancient Celtics and druids and often had the premonitions and more that changed the balance of many a battle. But the two had been the best of friends since their boyhood days, wandering in the woods around Philadelphia and had come to the wild uncharted territory several years back and were determined to live out their lives, exploring and discovering the wilderness.

Gabe, whose full name was Gabriel Alexander Stonecroft, was of different stock. A well-to-do family, made so by shrewd investments of his father, Boettcher Hamilton Stonecroft, a veteran of the Rev-olutionary war and Gabriel and his sister Gwyneth, lacked for nothing, including a university educa-tion. But when circumstances forced Gabe to flee Philadelphia, he was well outfitted from his father's extensive weapons collection and ample gold for the journey. His father's later death also provided him with an inheritance that was more than sufficient to last a lifetime. But the tall, blonde, broad shouldered well set-up man, who had been trained in the many ways of fighting and the use of weapons, had proven a perfect fit for a life of adventure in the mountains of French and Spanish Louisiana.

Gabe glanced at his friend, "What!? Don't I look like a likely leprechaun?"

Ezra shook his head as he continued down the trail, "Ain't never seen a leprechaun that's what, over six-foot tall!"

"Ahh, so you have seen one o' the wee creatures of the woods! And where might that have been, b'gosh an' b'gorrah?"

"What is leprechaun?" asked the lanky youth that walked between the two men. He was Two Drums, a *Nez Percé* that had been taken by the Blackfoot and escaped, then found by Gabe and his wife, Cougar Woman. Taken in after the raid by the Blackfoot and the retribution brought by the Salish, Two Drums had spent the winter with them, learning and sharing the ways of his people. Gabe had agreed to take the youth back to his people when warm weather returned and this day was showing the retreat of winter and the arrival of spring.

Gabe glanced to Ezra and said, "You're the one that claims to be Irish, you explain it."

Ezra shook his head, laughing and motioned Two Drums close, put his arm around his shoulder and as they walked toward the small lake that nestled in the bottom of the valley and began with, "Long ago and far away, in an enchanted forest, there lived a family of little people."

Gabe chuckled as he led the way to the edge of the shoreline at the deeper end of the lake. A thin sheet of ice still clung to the edges, showing thin as little ripples splashed against it. Far out, a big golden trout broke the surface, snatching at a mayfly, the first of the hatch. He dropped his blanket roll that held a fresh set of buckskins and long johns and started stripping off his duds. With a chunk of lye soap bundled in his dirty duds, he took the bundle in arms, got a running start and jumped into the cold deep water. He bobbed to the top, "Whoooeeee! It's cold!" he shouted as Ezra and Two Drums were stripping down.

Gabe kicked into the shallower water, touched the bottom and with shoulders above water level, began scrubbing the long johns and tunic and britches of buckskin. Ezra and Two Drums splashed into the water with a shout of their own and each began their own scrubbing. Once the clothes were done, the water was growing murky with soap, but they finished a thorough scrubbing of their bodies and hair, then waded to the shore, grabbing up the blankets to dry off and quickly get dressed. The cold air from the snowcapped peaks encouraged their haste as the chattering men scrambled into their duds.

As Gabe sat and stretched to put his moccasins on, movement at the edge of the trees on the far side of the valley caught his attention and he reached for his Ferguson rifle, never taking his eyes off the tree line. He grinned, then nodded in that direction, "Looks like we got comp'ny!" A shadow moved just inside the tree line and they saw a black bear stretch to full height on her hind legs, looking at the creatures at the edge of the lake. Then a sound that resembled a squealing bark or meow, came from behind her and two toddling cubs peered around their mother. She dropped to all fours, swatted one of the cubs and moved back into the timber.

"She's early!" stated Ezra, wrapping his sash around his middle and replacing his war axe and scabbarded knife.

"Like somebody else I know!" said Gabe.

"Will she be done yet?" asked Two Drums.

"Ha! A woman takes her time and a baby is even worse!" declared Ezra. "I know! Grey Dove has done it twice already and it's different each time! That's why they kicked us out!"

Gabe shook his head as he was reminded of what his woman was going through while they were cavorting in the lake.

***

"Uhnnnnahh!" grunted Cougar Woman. She was in a heavy sweat as she struggled to move beside the bed, breathing irregularly and shaking her head as she looked at Grey Dove. "It's early! I know it's early!" she gasped, both hands on her belly, glaring with a big question at her friend and fellow Shoshone.

"They come when they want to, when they're ready!" answered Dove, encouraging the new mother-to-be.

Cougar Woman was happy to have Grey Dove with her in the cabin, for it was not unusual for a woman of the Shoshone to walk into the woods, grab a sapling and squat to have her baby, unassisted. But this was the first time for Cougar Woman, who had been a proven warrior and war leader of her people, the *Tukkutikka* band of the Shoshone and had thought she might never be a mate and mother until she met the man known as Spirit Bear who had proven to be a greater warrior than she thought possible. Now he was her husband, Gabe, and she was proud to walk beside him.

In the room apart from the women, a toddler was running and giggling, playing with Little Owl, the Salish girl who chose to stay with the two couples after she was rescued from the Blackfoot by Gabe and Cougar Woman. She sat on the floor, arms extended as she smiled and watched the little one, Chipmunk, run to her and fall into her arms. Chipmunk was the first child of Ezra and Dove and bundled nearby in a cradle board was the newest addition, Squirrel, a girl that arrived just a month ago and the joy of her mother's eyes. Little Owl had stayed with the two couples to learn to read and know more about the God of the Bible that she had been introduced to, along with the other Salish youngsters rescued from the Blackfoot by Gabe and Cougar Woman. Although she had enjoyed the winter stay and had learned much of the ways of the white man and his friends, she was anxious to return to her people. But as she thought of her people, she also thought of Two Drums, the *Nez Percé* young man that had become her best friend. She smiled as she thought of him, letting the many other thoughts mingle and stir her mind as to the possibilities of a future together.

Chipmunk plopped onto her lap, reached up with tiny fingers to grab a handful of hair and tug, bringing Little Owl's attention back as she grabbed his hand, "Ow! You little stinker!" She picked him up and sat him on her hip as she walked to the room to join the women.

Cougar Woman looked up as Little Owl stepped through the door, then arched her back, her hand at her hip and started groaning again. She grabbed the post at the foot of the bed with her free hand and dropped her head as the pain swept over her. She grimaced as she looked to Dove, nodding toward the bed, and Dove took her elbow to help her negotiate the few feet to the edge of the bed for her to be seated and lay back. Dove motioned for Little Owl to take the toddler and leave, and then helped Cougar lift her legs to the bed.

2 / ADDITION

"Look at that! That boy doesn't miss a thing! Watch those eyes follow anything that moves and that look, you'd think he was a cougar or a lynx or a bobcat gettin' ready to take down his quarry!" declared Ezra, watching the newborn in his daddy's arms.

Gabe grinned and glanced at Cougar Woman lying on propped up blankets and stuffed pillows, smiled at her and back to Ezra, "So, looks like it's payback time! I hung a handle on your two, so I reckon it's up to you, Uncle Ezra."

Ezra put an arm around Dove as she held her newborn to her breast, beamed proudly at his new daughter and looked back at Gabe, standing beside the bedstead, gently rocking the attentive infant side to side. "You know, I think I done did! Just the way he's already payin' such close attention to ever'thing, he's a little Bobcat, that's what he is, a Bobcat!"

Gabe handed the little one back to his momma, sat on the edge of the bed and asked, "What do you think? Bobcat?"

Cougar Woman smiled, "It is fitting," she responded, then busied herself as she helped the boy take his milk. The women looked at one another, both brimming with pride and joy and Cougar smiled as the toddler, Chipmunk stood beside his mother, watching his little sister take her nourishment. The boy reached out to tenderly touch the infant, smiling up at his mother. Then with a soft word from Little Owl, the toddler made his way to the girl and the two went into the main room to join Two Drums and resume their play.

Ezra looked at Gabe, "Our family seems to be growing!"

"So, how're we gonna do any discoverin' and explorin' with all these young'uns?" responded Gabe, chuckling.

Cougar said, "We will go when and where you want to, no reason to delay!"

Gabe looked back at his woman, who sat with a stern look on her face, "Don't we need to stay home a while till they get a little older?"

"Why?" asked Dove.

Gabe looked from the women to Ezra, "I just thought . . ."

Both women were shaking their heads, a touch

of a smile tugging at the corners of their mouths as they looked at their men. Dove said, "We have cradle boards for the little ones and Chipmunk will ride with his father," nodding toward Ezra, who lifted his eyebrows in surprise, "and they," nodding toward the newborns, "will learn the ways of their people from the first day."

"So, that's how it is, huh?" asked Gabe. Both women nodded in agreement and Gabe looked at Ezra who shrugged his shoulders. "Then, I reckon we need to make preparations for the journey to take those two," nodding toward the other room where Two Drums and Little Owl sat watching Chipmunk, "back to their people."

***

"Look!" said Little Owl, pointing to a small cluster of low growing plants in a gravelly patch. Small white buds showed, about to burst open, and Little Owl added, "The *speam,* bitterroot, is starting to bloom. It will be ready to soon!"

"That little thing?" asked Gabe, twisting around in his saddle and pointing to the little cluster. "Do you eat the whole thing?" He looked from Cougar Woman to Little Owl as they rode two abreast on the tree hugging trail. Little Owl and Two Drums were behind Gabe and Cougar, who were leading a pair of packhorses.

"No, just the root. It is very special to my people. The women will have a great harvest, sometimes the whole village moves to be close to the bitterroot. All the roots are taken before the chief and he will pray for the harvest and for the people. My people believe there is great power in the root, it keeps sickness away and gives strength to the people. Inside the white root, there is a little red core, and some believe that will stop a bear attack," explained an enthusiastic Little Owl.

"Where was that when I needed it?" mumbled Gabe, touching the bear claw necklace about his neck.

Gabe was aboard his big black Andalusian stallion, Ebony, that his father bought as a yearling from a passing Gypsy. Cougar Woman rode her strawberry roan gelding, Ezra his long-legged bay gelding and Dove was aboard her Buckskin gelding. Gabe and Cougar led the buckskin mare Gabe brought back from St. Louis and the Steeldust mustang as packhorses, while Ezra led the pack mule and Dove the spotted rump appaloosa mare. Little Owl and Two Drums were mounted on horses taken from the Blackfoot, Owl on a line-back dun mare and Two Drums aboard a dapple-grey gelding.

Gabe glanced at Cougar Woman as she looked at the face of the infant that was nestled in a blanket wrap at her breast. The empty cradle board was atop the pack on the buckskin mare and Bobcat had yet to experience the fur lined baby carrier. Gabe was proud of his woman and his newborn child and his mind went to his family thinking how great it would be if his mother and father could see their grandchild, but both had already passed away, the only comfort being that he knew both were in Heaven. It was his mother that first told him of his need to know Jesus as his Savior, but he had thought religion was not to be a part of his life, until the truth of a relationship with the Lord was shown him by Ezra and through his friend's counsel, he finally accepted Christ as his Savior. Gabe smiled at the thought, finding comfort in knowing that one day his family would be complete in Heaven.

"Hssst!" came the warning from Cougar who held out her hand to stop Gabe. He had allowed his thoughts to wander and the danger of complacency brought him instantly attentive. He looked where Cougar was staring, through a break in the trees toward the openness of the valley just below them. Five riders were angling across the valley, their direction would intersect the trail Gabe and company now followed. Gabe glanced quickly around, seeing they were in thick cover of the black timber, firs with branches hanging low, towering spruce and ponderosa that shaded the trees and spotty aspen groves just showing buds on bare branches.

With his rifle in hand he slipped to the ground and moved closer to the edge of the trees. He scowled as he looked at the small band. They were not painted and were leading a single packhorse with the carcass of a deer draped over his back. Another horse, empty, was led by the last of the warriors. Gabe was certain this was a hunting party, probably just a split-off group from a larger party, and judging by the attire and hair, he believed they were Salish. He turned and motioned to Little Owl to join him and waited as she slipped to the ground and quietly came to his side. He nodded to the five riders, and softly asked, "Salish?"

Little Owl went down on one knee, moving side to side to look at the men, frowning as she looked, then a slow smile began to split her face as she turned to Gabe, "Yes. The one in the lead looks like Red Hawk."

Gabe grinned, remembering his time with the son of Spotted Eagle, the boy who came to warn them of the raiding Blackfoot and joined him and Cougar Woman to rescue several of the captives. At the time, the boy, about twelve summers, was an unproven warrior, but his time with Gabe and Cougar Woman earned him his marks and even though young, he was accepted as a proven warrior by his people. Gabe stood and whistled the hoarse extended scream of a red-tailed hawk. He watched as the leader of the group suddenly reined up and turned to look his direction, a scowl on his face.

The scream he heard would normally come from high above, not from the trees and Red Hawk searched the trees for the source of the call, a call that was also used by other Natives to signal their warriors. Gabe watched as the young man turned his horse to face the trees, showing his rifle that lay across the withers of his mount. Gabe mimicked the short chirps of a young hawk, then followed it by another extended hoarse scream, followed by his throaty laughter as he called out, "Red Hawk!"

The young man broke into a smile and gigged his horse toward the trail at the edge of the trees, recognizing the voice of his friend, Spirit Bear.

3 / SALISH

"Spirit Bear! It is good to see you!" declared a grinning Red Hawk, looking at the others in the mixed band. "A'ho Black Buffalo!" he said loudly, lifting his hand high to greet Ezra. He lowered his voice as he spoke to Gabe, "I see you have added to your lodge! A pair of papooses and the other one, a Blackfoot?"

Gabe shook his head, "No, he's *Nez Percé*. He was taken by the Blackfoot three summers ago and had escaped when we took the last of the raiders. Cougar Woman and I caught him trying to take our horses, but when we found out he was not Blackfoot, he decided to stay the winter with us. We'll take him to his people after we visit your village," explained Gabe as they walked back to the others.

"My father will be pleased to see you. He is with the other hunters; we will join him soon."

"So, how is Spotted Eagle?" asked Gabe, remembering the times spent with the Salish war leader as they bickered over the breeding of his mares.

"He is good. The wounds have healed, and he will soon take another woman."

Gabe paused, looked at Red Hawk, "Why that rascal! But I s'pose all the available women in the village were lookin' to move into his lodge after your mother crossed over."

"It is the way of my people. The family is important and there were many women that had lost their men in the raid by the Blackfoot. Our warriors are bound by our ways to provide for those without a man. It is a good way," surmised Red Hawk. As Gabe stepped beside Ebony, Red Hawk swung aboard his appaloosa and reined around, motioning to his hunters to lead the way on the oft-used game trail.

The sun was nearing its zenith when the hunters in the lead dropped from the trees into a clearing where several others waited. A blazing fire held strips of fresh meat hanging above the flames, horses were hobbled on the new grass and six Salish warriors were lounging by grey barkless trunks of long dead pines. When the reclining Spotted Eagle saw the other riders, he frowned and stood, looking past his son and the other hunters to a familiar face that made him smile and step forward, "Spirit Bear, my brother, you come to visit!"

Gabe slipped to the ground, greeted Spotted

Eagle with a grin and clasped forearms, slapping
his shoulder with his free hand. "Spotted Eagle! It is
mighty good to see you! Last I heard you were layin'
around your lodge havin' some widow wimmen
take care of you!"

The war leader grinned, motioning the newcomers
to step down. "Red Hawk, cut some more meat for our
friends," he directed as Red Hawk went to the hanging deer carcass. Eagle looked at Cougar Woman with
the blanket baby carrier and the top of the head of the
newborn showing with his thick patch of blonde hair.
He glanced at Gabe, back at the baby and said, "You
had a warm winter I see!" He grinned, then caught
sight of Dove with her new addition and laughed at
Ezra, "And Black Buffalo, you also spent much time in
your cabin!" The men laughed and seated themselves
on the remaining log, the women by their sides and
Spotted Eagle nodded toward the appaloosa pack
horse, "I see the mare you traded for is also with a
big belly, like those back at the village. Your black,"
nodding toward Ebony who was picketed with the
other horses of the bunch, "has done well."

Eagle had noticed the new additions to their group
and nodded, "Is that Little Owl?"

Cougar Woman answered, "Yes, she is a young
woman now and has learned much and taught much
as well. She has a good mind," tapping her forehead
as she spoke, "and will be a good teacher of the young

of the Salish people."

"And the one with her?" asked Spotted Eagle.

"He is of the *Nez Percé* and we are taking him back to his people. He was stolen by the Blackfoot," stated Gabe, reaching for a strip of freshly broiled venison steak.

***

Lances of gold shot heavenward from the descending sun as the hunting party and visitors rode into the village of the Salish. Many recognized Gabe and company, greeting them, walking beside them as they rode to the central compound of the camp. The leader, Plenty Bears, and his wife, Grasshopper, stood before their lodge, watching the returning hunters and others. When the chief recognized Gabe, he grinned and lifted his hand in welcome. They had fought together and shared meals, binding their friendship and the chief made them all welcome. "We will feast tomorrow!" declared the chief as he motioned the others to take the visitors to their lodge.

A scratch at the entry of their guest lodge prompted Gabe to call, "Enter!"

Spotted Eagle stepped through the doorway of the hide tipi, "I brought some cuts of fresh meat for your meal," he declared, handing a bundle to Cougar Woman as she knelt by the fire, readying things to prepare a meal. She smiled and nodded as she accepted the offering, setting it to the side as she placed the coffee pot on the stone near the flames.

Gabe had motioned Eagle to be seated and as he made himself comfortable, Gabe asked, "It looked like your people were getting ready to move or something, what is happening?"

Eagle smiled as he leaned back, "It is the time to gather the *speam,* or bitterroot. Tomorrow will be the time for digging the bitterroot. Because they are near, the women will dig, but the men will also go to protect them. It will be a special time and will start with Plenty Bears praying for the bitterroot and the people. It is the first feast of the growing time."

"Is that the feast Plenty Bears mentioned?" asked Ezra.

"Yes, but it will also be a feast because of our friends and visitors," answered Eagle.

A sudden scratch at the entry preceded a familiar face as Little Owl stepped in followed by another. She stood aside and motioned to the man, "I want you to meet my father's brother, Raven Walking." She pointed out each of the others, giving their names as she motioned. Gabe directed them to be seated and Little Owl just nodded as she said, "Raven Walking has taken a mate and they have offered for me to stay with them," she began as Raven nodded beside her, "but," she paused as she dropped her head, "he does not want me telling the others what I have learned."

Gabe frowned as she spoke, looking from Raven to Little Owl, with a glance to Cougar Woman. Cougar looked to Spotted Eagle, "Is it not allowed for Little Owl to teach the others what she has learned?"

The war leader asked, "What has she learned?" looking from Cougar to Little Owl.

Cougar nodded to the girl to let her tell, "I have learned the language of the white man, the Shoshone, the Blackfoot and the *Nez Percé*. I have learned the tracks of the white man in his book, the Bible and I have learned about the God of Heaven, as others that were captives learned, like," she nodded to Spotted Eagle, "your sons Red Hawk and White Feather. These have asked me to learn these things so I could teach them to make our people strong."

Spotted Eagle frowned, looking from Raven Walking to Little Owl and Cougar Woman, then asked Cougar, "Did you teach these things?"

Before Cougar could answer, Gabe spoke up, "We all taught one another. Little Owl taught us of your tongue," then nodding to Two Drums, "he taught us of the *Nez Percé* tongue and the Blackfoot. We taught them of the Shoshone language and the tracks in the book that tells of the Great Spirit that we know as God."

"Is it this God that makes you strong?" asked Eagle.

Gabe smiled, "God is the Creator of all things and

all people and yes, He gives us strength for every day and helps us in all we do."

Before he could continue, Little Owl interjected, speaking to Spotted Eagle, "Do you not remember the words of the prophet, Shining Shirt, that had a vision of men coming in long black robes to teach us of a new way to pray?"

Spotted Eagle frowned, "Yes," and he looked from her to Gabe and Ezra, "but not of a black man in the skins of the deer."

"But, when we first saw Spirit Bear," nodding to Gabe, "He had a long black bearskin coat, like the prophet told and he taught us a new way to pray."

Eagle scowled, looking from Little Owl to her Uncle and to Gabe. "This is something for Plenty Bears and the council. We will talk of this soon," he declared, ending the discussion.

Little Owl looked to Raven Walking and they turned to leave, but Little Owl spoke to Cougar Woman, "Do not leave without talking," her eyes pleading for her friend to stay. Cougar smiled and nodded, then watched her young friend leave the lodge.

4 / FEAST

"Oh, Great Creator," began chief Plenty Bears, standing with uplifted arms before the gathered people of the village, his eyes to the heavens, "we have seen the blossoms of the *sýeýeʔ* and we welcome the first visitor of spring, the *speam*, the bitterroot. We are thankful for the return of the bitterroot, and we give thanks for all the foods of this year. Our women go now to dig and the men go to protect, that we might have a great harvest of this great medicine. Let this be your way as you give this to keep sickness from our people. Thank you our Creator." He dropped his eyes to the many women that made up most of the crowd, then spoke to them, "You women, you bring your food, whatever you got, the bitterroot needs something, like children, to go with it, berries, meat, make this a great feast!" He nodded to the group to dismiss them and the chatter among the women started immediately, as they gathered their baskets and blankets and started for the fields.

Little Owl, Cougar Woman and Grey Dove were with the new bride of Raven Walking, Fox With No Tail. She had been among the women that watched the growth of the bitterroot and led the little group along the tree line to the gravelly slope where the small mostly white blossoms of the bitterroot covered the ground. The women were excited as they dropped to the ground to dig at the roots of the mountain delicacy. The men that accompanied them were standing to the side, away from the blossoms, some seeking shade from the nearby trees. Gabe, Ezra and Two Drums had come along as some of the protectors, but mainly out of curiosity about the big event.

The raw roots were unpalatable, but once the outer husk was peeled off to reveal the pale core, the roots would be baked in the coals or added to the pots of many stews and more that would be prepared for the feast. Using sharpened sticks, knives, carved spoons and any other thing that could be used to dig, the women were seated or on their knees as they enthusiastically dug for the roots, as excited as a child with their first mud puddle and were talking and jabbering all the while. This was not just a time of harvesting roots, this was a social time when the women could sit and talk or in many cases, gossip, to their heart's content.

When the sun was at its zenith, everyone went to the shade of the nearby tree line, carrying their parfleches of roots and their brought-along foodstuffs for their mid-day break. While they ate, the women peeled off the outer layer of the roots to reveal the pale core, discarding the peel and placing the treasured roots in their parfleche. By mid-afternoon, the harvest was complete and the people returned to the encampment of the village. Grasshopper, the wife of the chief, spread a blanket before the lodge of the chief and the women filed by, adding their harvest to that of the others. When the women were finished, the blanket was covered and the roots piled over two feet high. The chief stood before the pile, nodding and smiling, then to the women, "It is good. We," nodding to the leaders gathered near his lodge, "will pray for this," waving his hand over the pile of bitterroot, "as you prepare the feast." He turned to enter his lodge, followed by the other leaders that had marks or stripes for the deeds they had done and honors they gained.

Gabe noticed Spotted Eagle and Two Medicines, his brother, both followed the chief into the tipi with the other leaders. Gabe turned to Ezra, "How 'bout we go check on our horses?"

"Sounds reasonable," answered Ezra, motioning to Two Drums to join them.

The three walked to the back edge of the village where the horses grazed in the valley above the camp.

Watched over by several young men, some mounted, others stationed about, the herd of the encampment included the horses of Gabe and company. As they neared, Gabe spotted Ebony, the other horses near and saw the big black tossing his head as he saw his friend approach. The stallion with the long flowing mane and tail, arched his neck and tossed his head as he walked to Gabe, then stretched out his nose for the familiar touch. Gabe spoke to his horse as to a friend, "Hey big boy! How ya' doin'?" and stroked his neck.

Ezra had spotted his bay and the other horses and went to his gelding to greet him as he watched Two Drums seek out his dapple grey. Ezra called out, "They all look good! Happy too!"

"Yeah, I noticed Ebony sniffin' around a couple mares over there, but I don't think anything's gonna happen. I see that pepper-butt mare of mine has renewed her acquaintance with the others," nodding in the direction of a cluster of mares, most appaloosa, that held the other mares that were bred by Ebony.

"So, you gotta foal comin' outta one o' them, don'tcha?"

Gabe chuckled, "Yeah, the deal was two colts would be mine and two would be Spotted Eagle's, but I traded him outta that mare," nodding to the appaloosa with the spotted blanket on its rump, "so that just leaves me with one more. Red Hawk said he's gonna do the trainin' on the other colts."

"He'll prob'ly do a bang-up job, he's a good young man."

"Ummhmm, I think you're right about that."

Gabe glanced toward the village and saw Spotted Eagle approaching, waved, and turned back to stroke the face and neck of his black. When Eagle arrived, he said, "After the chief had the prayer for the bitterroot and the people, we talked about Little Owl and Raven Walking."

Gabe frowned as he looked at his friend, suspecting what he was about to hear would not be good, but he listened as Eagle continued.

"It is the right of Raven Walking to forbid her to teach or even speak to the others about what she has learned this winter. We cannot make it otherwise. If there was other family that would take her in, that would be allowed, but she has no other family," explained Spotted Eagle.

Gabe saw Two Drums start to speak and frowned at him to stop him, causing the young man to step back and remain silent. Gabe asked Eagle, "What is to keep her from becoming her own woman and become a mate of a warrior?"

"If she has accepted Raven Walking as her head, then it would be up to him. She has yet to make that known and with her father and mother gone, the decision would be hers."

Gabe caught the movement of Two Drums from

his peripheral vision, saw him begin to smile and turn away, then Gabe said, "If she were to be joined with another that was not of this village or your people, would she still be welcome in your camp?"

"Yes. Among my people, the man joins the family of the woman and moves into her lodge. If the man is of another people, he must avow his loyalty to our people."

Gabe nodded, understanding, and added, "I will talk to Cougar Woman, who has been like a mother to Little Owl. Perhaps there is a way that might make things right."

Spotted Eagle grinned, glanced toward Two Drums, "I thought that might be the way of things," as he turned away, he called over his shoulder, "The feast will begin soon. You are to join me." Gabe waved and nodded as he watched Spotted Eagle walk away, returning to the village.

Ezra and Two Drums came near Gabe as Ezra asked, "So, what does this mean for Little Owl?"

"That will be up to her. She has to make the choice to either stay with her uncle and her people, or . . ." he glanced at Two Drums. Then turned to face the young man, "I know you and Little Owl have been well, close to one another. But you are both still young yet."

"Yes, but I am a warrior," he declared, puffing out his chest, "I have proven myself in battle. By the way of my people and even the Blackfoot, that is all that must be done to prove yourself worthy of taking a mate!"

Gabe and Ezra both grinned, as Ezra spoke up, "It ain't just the takin' of a mate, you've got to take care of 'em. You know, provide a lodge, food, hides for clothing, all that and defend 'em against whatever."

Two Drums scowled, "Two Drums can do all that!" he declared.

Gabe looked at Ezra, letting a grin split his face, "You ain't gonna win that argument, my friend. Might as well save that for another day."

Gabe looked at Two Drums, "How would your people feel about you taking a wife from the Salish?"

"That is up to me, they do not concern themselves with these things," he answered, but his expression showed doubt.

Gabe added, "Don't forget, the last time you were with your people, you were just a youngster and probably had not thought about what it would be like taking a mate. There might be some things you don't know."

"This is true. But if Little Owl chooses to become my mate, will you still go with me to my people?"

"Yes, we will still be with you as we go to your people. But this is something you and Little Owl better talk about and I mean listen as well as talk, get my drift?"

"Two Drums understands."

"Then how 'bout we go back for that feast?" chimed in Ezra, rubbing his always hungry belly.

***

It was a festive time, feasting, dancing, storytelling and more. As the festivities wound down, young couples had paired off and disappeared into the darkness, older couples went to their lodges, leaving the others to continue with the dances and more. Gabe and Cougar had sat watching as they talked about Little Owl and Two Drums. Cougar Woman said, "She wanted to teach her people, the young ones that were taken with her and prayed with her, wanted to learn from Little Owl," she pleaded.

"Yes, I know. But the way of her people has limits within the family. Is it any different with your people?"

"No, but," she shook her head, "she is also young, maybe too young to become a mate of a warrior and that would be the only way she could become a teacher of her people."

"Even if that man is Two Drums?"

Cougar Woman frowned, "He is young also!"

"Ummhmm, but I think both of 'em have been thinking about joining."

"Perhaps, but . . ."

"I know. I was hopeful she would be able to help her people come to know the Lord also, but perhaps

He is opening the way for the Nez Perce'. Either way, it will be up to you to tell her, if Two Drums hasn't already talked about it," he nodded toward the drummers, where Two Drums and Little Owl sat just beyond the line of dancers.

Cougar Woman looked where he indicated, then back to Gabe, "We will know soon."

5 / JOURNEY

Gabe led the way west, Wolf at his side, away from the village of the Salish, bound for the unknown lands where they hoped to find the people of Two Drums, the *Chupnit-pa-lu*, as Cougar Woman called them. "My people called them the People of the Pierced Noses, but when I traveled with my father on the trade journeys, I never saw any with pierced noses."

"We are the *Nimíipuu*, or The People," declared Two Drums, riding beside Little Owl as they followed Gabe and Cougar Woman.

"I think just 'bout every tribe refers to themselves in their own tongue as, The People. It's usually because in ages past, they only knew of their own and of course thought themselves as the only people," explained Gabe. He looked at Cougar Woman, "So if they don't have pierced noses, how come the French call 'em *Nez Percé?*"

Two Drums spoke up, "My father said there was a time when they did pierce their noses, like the people toward the setting sun, called the Chinook."

"So, the name kinda stuck, huh? Well, that happens a lot, there's been a lotta folks get monikers hung on 'em they don't like."

The trail they followed shouldered the small run-off creek in the bottom of the narrow valley. Bound almost due west, the hills on the south were heavily timbered with a variety of conifers, but the hills with south facing slopes were mostly bare, save grease wood, sage and cactus, interspersed with tufts of buffalo grass. While the valley bottom was green and pleasant as the travelers often jumped mule deer, coyotes, fox and an occasional bunch of elk. The valley opened to show a fork and Gabe pointed Ebony to the north branch. He glanced at Cougar Woman, "Spotted Eagle said this is easiest and takes us to the headwaters of the Bitterroot River. We'll follow it a ways, prob'ly till dusk or so, then take a bit of a trail that'll put us into them high mountains, yonder," pointing to the west to the line of snowcapped peaks that paraded to the north.

Two Drums eagerly added, "Yes, and beyond those mountains is the land of my people!" He smiled broadly as he looked from Cougar Woman to Little Owl. Raven Walking, Little Owl's uncle, had refused to let Little Owl share what she had learned with the other youngsters of the Salish people, believing the Salish young should only be taught the stories of their own people. Frustrated at his refusal, Little Owl chose to go with Two Drums to his people and perhaps become his wife. She smiled back at Two Drums, wondering how she would be received by his people. Although Two Drums had assured her she would be made welcome and his people would be happy she would join them, he also said he was certain she could teach the young of his village. But she was concerned because when Two Drums had been taken from his people, he was much younger and they might not even welcome him back, perhaps believing he had been corrupted by the Blackfoot, the dreaded enemy of the *Nimíipuu.*

It was nigh unto mid-day when the trail dropped from the narrow mountainous valley into the broader flat with the Bitterroot River. Although the river bottom was lush and green the hills to the north and west were barren and uninviting. Gabe's gaze quickly took in the desolate panorama and said, "I see why Spotted Eagle called this the badlands of the Bitterroot!"

"Looks to me like the only place that holds anything green is this valley bottom," commented Ezra as he stepped down from his bay and lifted Chipmunk from the saddle. He went to Dove, reached up to take the cradle board with Squirrel.

"You're right about that," added Gabe, also helping Cougar Woman with her cradle board, although it was empty. She preferred to carry the little one in her blanket carrier hung around her neck, giving the newborn easy access to his milk. She had explained to Gabe, "He will be in the cradleboard soon enough, but he came early and needs to get stronger." But Gabe knew she was unhindered in her duties even with the little one held close and he was not one to argue about anything concerning newborns, knowing it would just show his own ignorance. He smiled as he stood the cradleboard beside a rock, then he and Wolf took the horses to water.

"So, how long ya figger it'll take us to get Two Drums home?" asked Ezra, holding the leads to the horses as they drank deep of the waters of the Bitterroot.

"Don't rightly know. Spotted Eagle seemed to think we'd find some *Nez Percé* soon's we cross them mountains, yonder," nodding to the snow-capped peaks. "But we both know the natives aren't always where you expect them."

Two Drums led his and Little Owl's horses to water beside the others and heard Gabe speak of his people. He glanced at the men, "My people do not move as do so many others, like the Salish and the Blackfoot. Many of the villages have been where they are for a long time. The lodges are dug into the earth and covered with tule mats and earth, not like the hide lodges of the Blackfoot."

"Tule? What'chu callin' tule?" asked Ezra.

Two Drums looked around, knowing the plant was found in marshy areas and where they were beside the river, he was certain there would be tule nearby. After a quick once over, he nodded, "there!" pointing to a marshy area at a bend of the river. He handed the leads to Ezra and trotted to the area, plucked several of the long stems measuring about four-foot-tall and brought them back to the men. He handed one to each of them, explaining, "My mother would make these into mats to cover the floors and sleeping areas of our lodge. In the middle of the lodge would be the fire circle, but around the edges were the sleeping areas, above the level of the fire," he motioned with his hand demonstrating a shelf like image around the interior of the lodge, "that would be covered with these mats." He pointed overhead, "The underside of the roof was these mats and on top would be layers of sod to make the lodge solid."

He took the leads from Ezra, "But some lodges were made with wood frames and had these mats laid over the top, like the hide lodges of the Blackfoot and the Salish." He dropped his eyes to the water, thinking, remembering, then looked up, "I remember one lodge was very long and covered with these mats. Many families lived together in the big lodge."

"So, you think the village of your people might still be where it was when you were taken?" asked Gabe.

"Perhaps. I would like it to be so, but sometimes

they do move when the grass no longer grows and the seeds no longer grow and sometimes they go together as a village for *kooyit.*" he answered, rather wistfully.

"What's *kooyit?*" asked Ezra.

"Like the Salish when they went for the bitterroot, my people have a feast for the first time to go for the fish. It is the most important for my people, I remember the feasting, but most of all I liked the fishing. We made great nets and scooped the fish from the water. My father made me a net, just my size and we fished together."

"Well, I don't know if we'll get there in time for *kooyit,* but we won't get anywhere if we don't get at it!" declared Gabe.

They had stripped the gear from the horses and were rubbing them down with dry grass as they watered. Wolf splashed into the water, cooling off and drinking his fill. Once the horses had their fill, they could roll in the grass and were staked out to graze, while the meal was prepared and eaten. Two hours was the usual mid-day break and they were soon on the trail again. The narrow trail that bordered the shallow river often rode the shoulders of the dry hills. Hooves clattered on rocks, dust lifted at every footfall, horses' heads bobbed with every step and the riders lifted neckerchiefs to cover their mouths. The river and trail twisted through the maze of gulches, finger ridges and gullies. Dry gravelly beds showed where spring runoff had cleansed the many draws of debris, carrying the deadfall to the river and letting the deeper waters carry it away. Those same gullies, now devoid of any moisture, had become the lair of coyotes, bobcats and rattlesnakes.

Late afternoon saw the descending sun paint the snowcaps gold and orange, making silhouettes of the promontories holding the snowpack. The narrow valley of the Bitterroot River widened and offered the vista of the Bitterroot mountains standing before the travelers with an invitation of shimmering white against a golden sky. Gabe looked at Cougar Woman, "That's about as beautiful a stretch of mountains as I've ever seen."

The valley stretched out in a northwesterly direction, then rounded a knob from a finger ridge and bent due north, on a winding path that followed the meandering river. The valley was verdant and green, benefiting from the spring runoff of the higher mountains on the west. The valley showed as a wide hem of the skirt of timber at the edge of the foothills and a herd of elk lifted heads to look at the newcomers. The big bulls were just showing velvet antlers, but none of the majestic beasts were bothered by the group and dropped their heads to continue their graze. Gabe chuckled and said, "You better be glad we've already got plenty of meat, otherwise I'd be happy to have some fresh elk steak!"

"Do you always talk to the animals?" asked a grinning Cougar Woman, riding beside her man.

"Most of the time, they're usually better listeners than most people." He looked down at Wolf, trotting beside Ebony, tongue lolling to the side as he craned around to look up at Gabe. "Ain't that right boy? You understand, don'tcha?" Wolf seemed to nod as he turned back to watch the trail.

"And they never argue?" asked Cougar, smiling coyly.

"Well, now, I wouldn't say that. Them grizzlies now, they're right good at puttin' up a purty convincin' argument."

"Ain't that the truth!" declared Ezra from behind them.

Two Drums looked at Ezra, "You have argued with the grizzly?"

Ezra chuckled, "Both of us have!" nodding to Gabe.

"What happened?" asked Two Drums.

Ezra chuckled, slipped his thumb under his grizzly claw necklace and lifted it from his tunic to show the young man, "An' he's got one too!" nodding to Gabe.

"I wish to get one also!" declared the youngster.

"Don't get in no hurry to be doin' it!" advised Ezra.

As they settled in for the evening camp, Gabe lifted his eyes to the billowing clouds over the north end of the long range of mountains. He glanced to Ezra, "Those grey bottoms tell of a coming storm, we better make certain the horses are tethered well."

6 / INFERNO

Gabe stood beside the lean-to where Cougar and the others lay sleeping. Wolf had stirred him awake with his insistence that prompted a cold nose on Gabe's face. The night had been an uncomfortable one at best, the wind had picked up and coming off the snow caps it was chilly. But now he watched as black bellied clouds marched closer on spider legs of lightning. The rumble of thunder was felt as much as heard and Gabe knew they were in for a severe storm. They made their camp on high ground and he was not concerned with flooding, but there was something about this one that sent the crawlies up his back.

Ezra rolled out of his blankets, leaving the women and little ones under the lean-to and looked where Gabe was focused on and shook his head, "That's lookin' bad."

"Ummhmm, but you can see it's not droppin' a lot-

ta water. Usually we can see the wispy slanting skirt of
rain that comes from the clouds, but the only thing I
see is the lightning." And as if to prove his point a spider web of white tentacles chased one another across
the black sky, accompanied by the rolling thunder
that was felt by everything around them.

Gabe had been counting the seconds between the
thunder and lightning and said, "That storm's about
10 miles away. It'll be here soon."

Ezra turned toward the horses, but Gabe stopped
him with, "I checked on 'em, their snugged down and
close to one another. Those tall ponderosa'll give 'em
some cover, but . . ."

"Yeah, but! If that lightnin' hits close to 'em, ain't no
tether gonna hold 'em. They'll jerk that little juniper
right outta the ground." He paused and lifted his face
to the sky, "I can smell it! That's more lightnin' than
we've seen in a long time, like forever!" he declared as
the sky was split with another series of bolts.

The cool air on their faces caught their attention,
but Gabe said, "Feel that? That air is dry, not much
rain." Then his eyes flared wide and he leaned forward,
mouth open and lifted his hand to point, "Look!"

Gabe was spellbound and Ezra's eyes were wide
as the two looked at the unusual phenomenon before them. A blanket of mist that appeared to cover
the entire valley began to glow with a brilliant blue
luminescence. Gabe quickly stirred Cougar and Dove

awake to see the glow as it seemed to dance like a legion of fairies atop the grass and brush in the valley bottom. It slowly changed to a violet glow and the tips of trees at valley's edge seemed to be aflame with brilliance, glowing in the darkness. The big cloud rolled slowly toward them as lances of lightning danced at the edges. The spectacle seemed to hiss or buzz as it rolled along the edge of the winding river.

Cougar drew close to Gabe, "What is it?" she whispered, unable to take her eyes from the strange image.

"I think it's what's called St. Elmo's fire! I've heard of it bein' seen at sea by the sailors, but I've never seen the like before."

Two Drums asked, "Is it the *weyekins?*"

Gabe frowned and looked at Drums, "The what?"

"*Weyekins,* the little people of the forest."

"No, this is somethin' else," started Gabe, watching the light begin to fade and suddenly disappear. He looked around, from treetops to valley floor and it was as if nothing had appeared. While the storm still rumbled and lightning still pierced the darkness, the phenomenon of light was gone. He looked to the sky again, judged morning to be coming soon and suggested, "From the looks of things, that storm'll be on us soon, so you might wanna hunker down a spell, least till it passes." He glanced at Ezra, "Ya think the horses will do better if we bring 'em close and stay with 'em?"

"Prob'ly, at least we can try to keep 'em calm, you know, talk to 'em and such," answered Ezra.

The women, hearing the stirrings of the babies, turned away from the men and crawled back into the lean-to and set about feeding the now stirring newborns and Dove tucked the blankets around Chipmunk. Neither knew what to say about what they had witnessed but turned to their own thoughts as they nursed the babies.

As the men walked to the horses, Gabe asked Ezra, "You feelin' anything?"

Ezra frowned, "What'chu mean?"

"You know, those premonitions you get now and then, anything?"

"Can't say as I do, why?"

"I'm gettin' mighty uncomfortable 'bout somethin'. Don't know what, but I was feelin' it even before the light in the valley."

"Maybe that was what it was about," suggested Ezra.

"No, I don't think so," he concluded, shrugging his shoulders as he began to loosen the tether on the black and Cougar's roan. He gathered the leads for the two pack horses together with those of the black and roan and started back to the lean-to. Ezra and Two Drums followed close behind, leading the other horses. Gabe loosely laced the leads together, giving added anchorage to the leads with each of the horses tied to the others. They had been a little skittish with the thunder and lightning, but they were used to storms in the mountains and did not seem too riled.

The men slipped on their capotes, and although the wool garments would not shed the rain, the wool would still keep them warm. They moved through the horses, speaking softly, stroking each one, trying to keep them calm. Gabe spoke to Ezra, "A cup of hot coffee would sure go down good 'bout now."

"Ummhmm, but unless you can slap a rope on the lightning to heat the water for you, I'm afraid you're gonna hafta wait, same as me!" answered Ezra.

The storm moved overhead, the rain of fine droplets did little more than settle the dust, but the lightning prevailed and the thunder rolled across the sky as the storm marched past. Their camp was on the south side of the mouth of the valley that would be their route over the mountains, a little clearing among the thick timber on a bit of a shoulder above the runoff creek in the bottom. With no more rain that fell, they were unconcerned about flash flood waters and at Gabe's suggestion, "How 'bout a quick breakfast and we hit the trail?" everyone hove to and they were soon lined out and pointed west through the deep cut between the sky scratching peaks of the Bitterroot.

The sun was at their back and a steady breeze was pushing them deeper into the notch when Ezra called from the rear of the line, "Hey, you smell that?"

Gabe reined up, turned to look back down the line, lifted his head, "Yeah! Smoke! And lots of it? See anything?" he hollered back.

The trail followed the stream and bent a little to the northwest, obscuring the view of the valley they left and the mouth of the canyon. Ezra twisted around in his saddle, stretched high in his stirrups, and with a hand on the cantle of his saddle, he craned to see further. "Smoke! Comin' our way! That wind is pushin' it to us!"

"Can you see any fire? Mighta started from the lightnin'!"

Ezra twisted around again, then reined his horse around and started back down the trail. Within a few seconds he came back at a run, "Fire! Get a move on! It's comin' fast!"

Gabe slapped legs to the big black, saw Wolf take off at a run and followed after him. The pack horse lead jerked him around, but he held tight and stretched out the neck of the steeldust mustang pack horse and watched as Cougar did the same with her roan and buckskin pack horse. The trail widened and Gabe reined up, pulled to the side and waved Cougar past. "Find some water, a lake or somethin'!" he shouted as she passed, nodding her head and stretching out her arm behind her to urge the buckskin packhorse close.

Gabe waved the two youngsters past and motioned for Dove to follow close behind. She had the appaloosa mare as a pack horse and the appy was pushing her buckskin up the trail. Ezra was close behind her, Chipmunk on the saddle before him, and the mule pushing them. Gabe grinned and fell in behind the rest.

It was an all-out run to flee from the raging flames that were fed by the dry timber and the howling wind that blew through the valley as if funneled through a hose. The wind whistled, howled and moaned and the flames licked their way through the brittle pines that stood so close together their limbs were inter-twined. Tongues of flame shot skyward as if licking at the bottoms of the clouds, impish fairies of flames danced from treetop to treetop, tiptoeing their way up the valley and laughing all the way like a crazed and screaming banshee.

The trail rode the bottom of the slope from the granite tipped peaks, shadowing the stream in the narrow bottom of the canyon. With steep talus slopes, granite slab slides and limestone cliffs, there was only one way out and that was straight through the canyon. But the fuel for the fire was plentiful with juniper shrubs, trees, fir and spruce trees and more. All the horses sensed and smelled the fire, adding fear to their flight. Hooves clattered on the rocky trail, leather creaked, horses grunted and people shouted encouragement to their mounts. Every animal was stretched out, manes and tails flying, lather foaming at the girths and riggings, each one reaching for another step, another league further away from the flames.

Gabe could hear the crackling and booming as the flames bounded up the narrow valley. Pine sap flared, deposits of sap exploded, skeletal branches stretched out with fiery fingertips, passing the torch to each of its neighbors and the roar filled the canyon. Gabe glanced back to see the towering dark grey cloud billowing up to the mountain tops and he slapped legs to the big black.

***

Cougar let her mountain bred roan have his head and dug heels to his ribs, even though she knew he needed no goading, but it was somehow necessary. She lay low on the neck of the gelding, mane slapping her face. She held the lead of the buckskin mare tight against her hip, seldom glancing back to the mare. Before her, she saw the valley make a sharp bend to round a massive granite knob that towered over the valley like a stone goblin, his face smashed in and appearing as a black ominous shadow. She goaded the roan into the shallow creek bottom to round the big monolith and kept to the creek as it twisted through some black timber. Then she saw a flat just above, heard that gurgle of a small waterfall and pushed the roan from the timber to follow a brushy trail to the top of the flat. There, just when it was needed, a small lake, shallow on the north edge with sparse brush and timber at that shore. Without hesitation, she gigged the roan into the water, following a paddling Wolf, dragging the buckskin mare pack horse behind.

Cougar was followed closely by both Two Drums and Little Owl, then with only an instant's hesitation, Dove came into the water with the appaloosa mare right behind. Soon, the lake was dimpled with horses, standing belly deep in the cool water, sides heaving and turning to look back down the flaming gorge. Gabe was the last one in the water and all turned around to face the conflagration that roared its way closer.

"You found a good one!" declared Gabe, looking to Cougar Woman, he nodded to the north bank, "That stuff there, if it burns at all, won't amount to much and we can get out over there where Wolf's waiting," pointing to the sloping bank on the northwest edge of the lake where Wolf was rolling his hide to free it of the water. Gabe had brought his one leg up and crossed it over the pommel of his saddle, leaning forward as they watched the approaching fire.

7 / CANYON

Sparks sailed overhead like the lightning bugs from Gabe's youth in the woods behind their home in Philadelphia, but these took flight and were carried by the howling windstorm made such by the blazing fire. The heat rolled up the valley like the blast furnaces of the blacksmith carrying the flames as the warriors of old when they charged the castles of their lords. The fire marched on legs of black stumps left behind as desolate reminders of the devastation, unhindered by terrain and fed unceasingly by the tinder of dry timber. The roar of the fire increased as it neared, sparks multiplied, the popping and booms of exploding trees added to the cacophony.

Gabe dropped his foot into the stirrup and lifted the reins on the big black. The horse was sidestepping, nervous and apprehensive as he unconsciously moved back away from the approaching flames, but the footing was uncertain and Gabe touched his heels lightly to move him forward, reaching down to stroke his neck and speak to him, giving him the reassurance of his control. The others mimicked Gabe, also reassuring their mounts, reaching out to touch the packhorses at their sides.

The flames had slowed at the point of the canyon where the granite monolith partially blocked the way, but the fire soon circumvented the knob, splitting as it took on both forks of the canyon. Gabe and company were about three hundred feet above the canyon bottom where the flames started climbing the canyon walls. From their vantage point, they saw that the south rim of the canyon held timber on the lower slopes, as the north slopes were mostly barren. The fire gobbled up the timber as it climbed like a voracious monster, eating everything in its path, the billowing smoke climbing high into the sky and blocking out the sun. The darkness preceded the flames that moved steadily toward the lake of refuge. The horses sidestepping away from the timber covered crag, watching the encroachment of the inferno. The low rocky bluff that dammed the lake was partially covered with scrub oak brush that flared and licked at the water's edge as it reached for the growth along the north shore. The taller timber that covered the south face flared into flames, but the low brush on the north side simmered, sputtered and had soon exhausted its supply of fuel.

They watched as the fire tried desperately to engulf the lake, drawing closer to one another, reaching out to touch each other, desperate for the comfort of company. Relief swept over them like a breath of fresh air as the fire sizzled out on the north shore. They looked back through the curtain of smoke as the flames consumed the trees on the south and soon found purchase behind them and began its race toward the end of the canyon almost two miles higher. Gabe motioned Ezra to lead the way onto the north shore where Wolf sat on his haunches inviting them to join him.

As the horses stepped on shore, each rider quickly slid to the ground, giving the horses their chance to shake off the excess water. Gabe looked at the others, "Anybody for starting a fire and cooking some lunch?" Cougar Woman reached for a rock to chuck at her man, picked it up and threatened, but when he laughed and shrugged, she smiled and dropped it, both happy to be alive and well and together.

Gabe looked at Ezra, "I don't think we'll be goin' anywhere for a while, at least till things cool off a little, so how's about we strip the horses and let 'em graze on this bit of grass the fire missed and maybe make us a camp. Don't reckon we need to worry 'bout no more fire since it done burnt everything!"

"Didn't it though," replied Ezra, then chuckled, "If you could only see yourselves now, you're all about as black as I am!"

Everyone looked at each other and laughed, shaking their heads and Cougar was the first to offer, "The water there is clean enough, but you might have to skim off some of the ash that's floating. Or wait till morning, it'll probably all be on the bottom by then."

***

It was a long day, even with an early start and made longer when most of the morning's trek was made through the ashes, still warm in places, from the fire that ripped through the canyons. By mid-day they made the crest and were out of the burn, the rest of the day easier, better trail and downhill all the way. By evening they bottomed out and came to the confluence of the run-off stream they followed from the crest and the river that Two Drums thought might be the Selway, or what some of the natives called Stripe River.

"Anybody else ready to get rid of all this ash and charcoal?" asked Gabe as he stepped down, letting the horses take their customary drink before stripping the gear.

His suggestion was met with laughter and shouts from everyone as they hurried to find their special place to strip and get in the water. The confluence offered a sizable backwater pool that was claimed by the women, leaving the men to tend to the animals, that once stripped of their gear, were led into the water by the men and rinsed down to rid their coats of the accumulated dust, ash and grime. When they were finished with the horses, the women had also finished and were coming from the willows in their fresh clean clothes, drying their hair with blankets and enjoying themselves after the refreshing bath.

Two Drums had readied a fire circle with a stack of firewood and readily followed the men into the backwater pool for their baths, each one eager to rid themselves of the day's soot and grunge. As Gabe lathered his hair, he commented, "Those are some trees, aren't they?" nodding toward the tall cedars that stood above the river bank. Towering more than a hundred feet high and some twice that tall, with a girth of four to five feet in diameter, the monster trees were bigger than anything the men had seen on their journeys.

"Ain't they a cedar of some kind?" asked Ezra.

"I think so, but they sure make a man seem mighty small, don't they?"

"They do that, for sure."

"My people use the inner bark to make rope, mats, and more. My father and the men of the village made a big boat from one, it would carry this many," said Two Drums as he held both hands out all fingers extended.

Gabe looked from the lad to the tree, "I can see that. That big'un there could make a canoe big enough to hold a lot more'n that."

***

The trail that shadowed the river and wound through the steep timbered mountains kept the group traveling for four long days before the mountains relaxed and let the weary travelers see foothills and open spaces. Two Drums smiled and said, "This is the land of my people." Shortly after the Selway merged with the Clearwater River, a wide bend offered a good camp for the group and Gabe led them to the edge of the trees at the mouth of a wide tree-lined gulley. As the men stripped the horses, Gabe nodded to the hilltop behind their camp, "I think I'm gonna climb up there and look around. We've been in the canyons so long, I'm needin' to see some wide-open country!"

***

When Gabe and Wolf mounted the knob, he sat down and pulled his scope from the case, looking around at the surrounding terrain. He frowned when he saw smoke spiraling from beyond the line of hills downstream from their location and with elbows on his knees, he steadied the scope for a better look. He grinned as he saw a village, exactly as Two Drums had described, several earthen dome lodges, some tipi types with tule mats covering them and three long houses, also covered with tule mats. Many cookfires burned outside the lodges, people busy with usual activities as children played and mothers cooked. Except for the type of lodges, it was little different than the many villages of the plains tribes. He looked at the village for a while longer, then gave a cursory once-over of the surrounding terrain until his eye caught something that riveted his attention.

Focusing in on the sight, Gabe discovered a camp, about three miles distant from the village, of what appeared to be that of traders. Several packs were stacked by the trees, horses were tethered and a cook-fire sent a wisp of smoke into the trees. The men were all in buckskins, except for two that had woolen shirts and britches held up by galluses. High topped boots were the favored footgear, and most had felt hats. *Looks to me to be some traders, probably from Hudson's Bay company. They look French or French Canadian to me.* He breathed deep, uneasy with what he saw, but after a last look at both the traders and the village, he rose and started back to the camp.

8 / KAM'NAKKA

"My people are near?" asked Two Drums as he heard Gabe tell of seeing the village. "Then we must go, now!" he declared, excitedly.

"No, it's late," he answered, lifting his eyes to the lowering sun that barely peeked over the horizon, sending colorful reminders of the end of day, golden lances against orange bottomed clouds. "We'll go first thing tomorrow, but I'm sure the women want to be ready to meet your people, especially Little Owl there," nodding to the young woman, already showing her concern about meeting the family of Two Drums.

"But, we could go now, the women come later!" offered Two Drums, anxious to see his people.

"Look Two Drums, we don't know yet if your family is here with this village and it's been more'n three years since you've been here and we don't know what they will do about us," he motioned to himself and the others, "they might not be too friendly with a bunch of strangers."

"My people will be friendly, I am with you and I am one of them," argued Two Drums, growing frustrated with the delay.

"Two Drums, we've visited with a lot of different people and one thing we know, we can't go riding into a village, uninvited, and expect to be received as friends. We need to approach slowly, peaceable and show the right respect. That can only be done in broad daylight. Now, let the women help Little Owl get outfitted, you do the same, coz, right now you look more like a Blackfoot than a *Nez Percé.*"

Two Drums stared at Gabe, frowning, then looked down at his leggings and breech cloth and moccasins, then back to Gabe, "I do look like a Blackfoot. I must change."

"Looks to me like the only thing you need to change is your moccasins and maybe do your hair up proper," said Ezra, noting the difference among the people. "Blackfoot have those black soled moccasins, and your hair there, that top knot is also Blackfoot."

Two Drums looked at Ezra, "Yes, my people have moccasins with beading and higher tops," he looked at the others footgear and nodded toward Little Owl, "like hers, only two parts. And the men do not have a topknot on their hair, it is flat, sometimes with a piece here," pointing to his forehead.

"Well, maybe Cougar Woman can help with the moccasins and Grey Dove can do somethin' 'bout your hair. I really don't wanna get shot 'fore we even get into camp," replied Ezra.

Two Drums dropped his head, "My people do not have many enemies, but they have fought with the Blackfoot, like when I was taken. But I remember my father telling of raids with the Shoshone and the Ute."

Gabe shook his head, "So, now you tell us! We coulda ridden into that village with our women, both of 'em Shoshone and find out your people are enemies with the Shoshone!" He looked from Two Drums to the women, both of whom were smiling and laughing and said, "You are riding right up front with me and if anybody gets shot, it'll be you!"

***

As the women started with Little Owl and Two Drums, Ezra and Gabe sat at the low fire, waiting for the coffee. Gabe looked to Ezra, "I also spotted what appears to be a camp of traders. Looked like French, probably with Hudson's Bay. Everything looked alright, but something's not sittin' well with me, I dunno."

"Well, no wonder. Our experience with Frenchies and their ways hasn't been too beneficial for any of us, especially after that bunch tried to take off with me'n the women. But they can't all be bad, can they?" asked Ezra.

"If we didn't have Two Drums and him all anxious to see his people, I think I'd just as soon hang back and wait to see what happens with the traders 'fore we try to meet up with the *Nez Percé.*"

"You know, you used to be a trusting soul, but now that you're gettin' older, not so much!" observed Ezra, looking at Gabe sideways and with a slight grin.

"Older?! I ain't no older'n you! And I ain't seen any grey hair on either of us!" he frowned, thinking. "How old are we anyway?"

Ezra frowned also, for it was not the way of the natives nor of those in the wilderness to be too concerned with ages and birthdays. Both men started remembering back to the time they left Philadelphia and Ezra said, "Uh, we were what, nineteen when we left Philly?"

"You were, but I had just had my twentieth birthday, remember?"

"Yeah, and we spent the first winter with the Osage, then . . ."

"Oh well, no matter," drawled Gabe, "I think it's only been about five years, but we've already lived two or three lifetimes since we came to the territories."

"So, who's president now?" asked Ezra.

"Last I heard, Thomas Jefferson was about to be put in office, but I'm not too sure how that came out."

"So, what do you want to do about these traders?"

"Reckon we just have to wait an' see, hopefully nothin'."

***

Gabe and Two Drums were at the front of the small band as they approached the village, Wolf trotting beside them. Four warriors stepped before them, arrows nocked on their bows, one with a lance held across his body to block the group from coming any closer. He saw Wolf, stepped back slightly then lifted his eyes to Gabe and asked in the language of the *Niimíipuu,* "Who are you, why have you come to our village?"

Gabe nodded, answering in their language as he had learned from Two Drums, "I am known as Spirit Bear. We come to bring one of your own," motioning to Two Drums, "back from his captivity with the Blackfoot."

Two Drums spoke quickly, "I am Two Drums, of the *Pikhininu* band. My father is *Hohots Llppilp,* Red Grizzly Bear. I was taken three winters past by the raiding Blackfoot," he spat the word Blackfoot as he glared at the warriors.

The men had recognized the name of Two Drum's father, looked at one another and back at Gabe and Two Drums, "Follow me, I will take you to our chief." Without waiting for a response, the holder of the lance turned and stepped off, expecting them to follow.

Although it was early morning, most had already finished with the first meal of the day and were busy with the typical activities of the native people. Children were playing a variety of games, most with little or no clothing, running barefoot and laughing, some saw Wolf and came closer, but kept their distance as they looked at the big wolf. Women were busy with hides, scraping, cleaning and more, one mother saw her child approaching the visitors and at the sight of Wolf, hollered at her son, making him stop. The boy stared at the visitors, looked at Wolf but showed no fear, just curiosity.

The smoke racks were different than what they were used to seeing, they were more like elevated racks with many strips of meat, mostly fish, hanging over the smoke pit. Tule mats hung at the sides to keep the smoke within the space of the racks. Men were busy with nets and weapons and most would glance up at the visitors, but showed little concern and continued with their tasks.

Gabe and company were taking in the sights of the people, pointing out the different lodges, tipis that were quite similar to those of the plains natives, but several that were covered with tule mats that didn't come all the way down, allowing the free flow of air underneath. The long houses covered with tule were different as were the earth lodges. As they neared the central compound, Gabe saw several men seated before a large tule covered tipi who stood as they neared. One man stepped from the others, a blanket over one shoulder held together by one hand. His straight hair hung past his shoulders and was parted on the sides and pulled back, except a portion that hung over his forehead, neatly trimmed and greased. His nostrils flared and he glared at the newcomers, glanced at Wolf, then looked to his warrior as the man told about the visitors.

"I am Twisted Hair, the leader of this *Kam'nakka* band of *Niimíípuu.* You speak our language?"

"Yes. I am Spirit Bear, this is my wife, Cougar Woman of the Shoshone. My friend," pointing to Ezra, "is Black Buffalo and his woman, also a Shoshone, is Grey Dove. We have brought Two Drums back to his people."

The chief looked from Gabe to Two Drums, "Who are your people?"

"I am Two Drums, of the *Pikhininu* band. My father is *Hohots Llppilp*, Red Grizzly Bear, my mother is Wind in her Hair. I was taken three winters past by the raiding Blackfoot."

The chief stepped closer to look at the young man, motioned him to get down and as he stood before him, nodded, "I knew your father. He has crossed over and is with our ancestors. Your mother, Wind in her Hair, is here, in our village, she came with us to join her sister at the last encampment." He pointed to the south end of the village, "Her tipi is there, by the trees. Go to her."

Two Drums looked from the chief to Gabe, glanced at Little Owl and motioned her to come with him. Then speaking to Gabe, "You and the others come soon?"

Gabe nodded and with a glance to the chief, asked, "May we step down?"

The chief nodded, waited for the others to step down, then said, "There is a place near the lodge of Wind in her Hair where you can camp. If you need a lodge, we have one. It is a good thing you do, to bring our own to us. You are welcome to stay with our village."

"We are grateful, Twisted Hair." He paused, considering, then added, "I spotted some white men camped on a flattop over yonder," pointing with his chin to the north, "I reckon they'll be paying you a visit. Traders I reckon."

"We know of them. Our warriors also told of your camp last night. The others have been there for one day before this."

Gabe nodded, and said, "We'll go to see the family of Two Drums."

The chief nodded, "We will talk again."

As they turned away, another warrior rode into the circle, swung down, and spoke to the chief, overheard by Gabe, "The traders come! There are this many," he held out two hands, all fingers extended. The chief nodded, motioned to the lance bearing warrior and the others to return to the edge of the camp to await the other visitors.

Gabe glanced at Ezra, then with Wolf at his side and Cougar Woman beside him, started to the far edge of the village. He looked at Ezra, "Did you hear?"

"You mean about the traders? Yeah."

Gabe shrugged, then added, "I'd like to know what goes on, there's just somethin'. . ."

"Not our concern," cautioned Ezra.

The lodge of Wind in her Hair was easily spotted, Two Drums, Little Owl and the woman were seated on blankets near the still simmering cookfire, animatedly talking and laughing. It was a pleasant scene, but a shadow of sadness was also present. When Two Drums saw the others coming, he stood and motioned them close. "Mother, these are my friends, Spirit Bear, Cougar Woman, Black Buffalo and Grey Dove." He turned to the other woman, "And this is the sister of my mother, Walks Softly."

The morning was spent renewing memories and getting acquainted. Wind in her Hair explained, "The father of my son has been gone since before the snows came. A raid by the Paiute. But he showed himself strong. He killed three Paiute before he was killed." She looked at Two Drums, "It is good to have my son back. I did not think I would ever see him again and now when he is needed the most, you have brought him home."

9 / TRADERS

"I'm telling you, if you can't keep your hands off the women, I will cut them off!" growled Adrien Lauren, the leader of the Hudson's Bay Voyageurs. A big, broad shouldered man who had been with the company for most of a decade and traveled much of Canada and New France, establishing trade with the natives. But he had never had so much trouble with any one man until now. "You've already cost us a bundle of furs with the Palus and the next time I'll just let the natives have their way with you!"

"Hehehe, might be worth it after I have my way with their women!" answered the burly, barrel chested, Bruno Berger. A mountain of a man, he was tolerated for his strength, for he alone could heft a full bale of pelts and hold it in place while others strapped it down to the pack frame. His smell was as big as his bulk and his face and neck was a mass of black, matted and bug infested hair, with two drool trails where tobacco turned the black to brown. He cared little for the pay, wanting only to have his way with any women, but his way always ended the life of any that fell into his clutches.

"You might think you're too big to hurt, but this," patting the pistol in his sash, "will leave a .62 caliber hole in your forehead just as easy as anyone's. And don't think I'll hesitate, 'cause if it comes to a choice of profits for the company and having you around, profits win every time!" declared Adrien Lauren.

Bruno turned away, grumbling and was followed by a mousy looking weasel faced runt named Henri Petit. The little one had a voice to match his twitch, long nose and patchy whiskers that made everyone think of him as the mouse he was, twisting, squeaking and twitching as he walked beside his hero and protector.

Adrien turned to Gaston Durand, his number two. Arrayed in a buckskin tunic over woolen britches and high-topped boots, his red sash matched the long feather in his wide-brimmed felt hat. He was the equal in size and experience to Lauren, yet was second in command, which suited him well, for he was never anxious to take charge nor take the blame for anything. Adrien asked, "Everything ready?"

"Oui. Those four," nodding to the four youngest of the bunch, "will stay at camp with the horses and the furs, the rest will come with us. We will have four packhorses loaded with goods, two more, empty to carry back the peltries."

"I need you to keep an eye on Bruno. We can't have any more problems like before."

"Oui, and what about Jean-Phillipe?"

Adrien smiled, "He's just a lover and none of his conquests have caused us problems, but it would be best if we kept all the men with us, rather than running free through the village."

"But someone needs to go through the village to get the people to come trade. If we do not, many will stay away and our trade will not be as good," pleaded Gaston.

Adrien thought a moment, he looked at his ledger, "Then you and Jean-Phillipe Fabron do the solicitations for trade, but trade only!" he cautioned, then added, "That leaves Bernard Moreau, Bruno and the mouse with me. Bernard and I will handle the trades, Bruno and Henri will do the hauling and packing."

"Then you will need to tell them before we leave, you'll get some arguments from Bruno and Henri," stated Gaston.

"I'll handle them, you just keep your eye on lover boy," cautioned Adrien.

***

The traders were met by the same warriors that greeted Gabe and company, but the leader, Adrien Lauren, spoke fluent *Niimiipuutímt,* the language of the *Nez Percé,* having traded with other bands of the people. "I come with greetings from chief Bird from the Light of the *Pikhininmu* band."

The traders were led to the central compound before chief Twisted Hair, who asked, "You bring greetings from Bird from the Light?"

"Yes Chief. We traded with his band a few days back, he said we should come to your band and make trade."

"Where is his camp?" asked the chief, suspicious of the traders.

"This summer they have moved their camp to the confluence of the Snake and the Palouse rivers, getting a bit close to the territory of the Palus people," explained Adrien.

"You trade now?" asked the chief, looking at the others and the loaded packhorses.

"We would like to, we have many things that your people like, beads, needles, cloth and more."

The chief nodded, motioned to the open area beyond his fire pit and turned back to his lodge. Adrien turned back to his men and began giving instructions about laying out the trade blankets and the goods, nodded to Gaston to take Jean-Phillipe and go into the village. Once the horses were unloaded, the mousy one, Henri Petit, was tasked with taking the horses from the village and picketing them on some graze. He motioned for Bruno to help him and Adrien did not object since there were a dozen horses to tend to, too many for one man.

Bernard Moreau was a quiet man, thin as a rail, over six foot tall with coal black hair and beard that had a streak of pure white that ran from the back of his head, down the side in front of his ear and down into the beard. A few were tempted to call him skunk, for he truly resembled one, but Bernard was quick tempered and as deadly as a viper and twice as fast, so he never gained that moniker. He was a smart and cunning trader and was bested only by Adrien himself. His drop shoulder muslin shirt, topped fringed buckskin britches and were split with a multi-colored sash that held a long bladed knife and tomahawk as well as a flintlock pistol that stood prominently at his middle, appearing to be as long and skinny as the man himself.

While Bernard and Adrien arranged the trade goods, Gaston Durand and Jean-Phillipe Fabron started into the village, greeting the people by sign, French and a smattering of the native tongue, encouraged the people to bring their trade goods, pelts, hides, dried roots and more, to the compound for trade.

Jean-Phillipe was an impressive figure with wavy black hair and beard, piercing black laughing eyes and a perpetual smile. He wore a muslin shirt over woolen britches tucked into tall moccasins and a red knit cap with a long fob that hung to his shoulder. His mellow voice and broad smile caught the attention of all the women and many responded flirtatiously and he always added his winsome way to the tete-a-tete. Gaston repeatedly prompted Jean-Phillipe to come along after him, but after the third interlude with a woman, Gaston shrugged and walked on, leaving Jean-Phillipe to his doings.

***

Gabe and company moved into the guest lodge, a tule covered tipi not far from the tipi of Two Drums mother and Gabe and Ezra heard the buzz among the people of the traders setting up their trades. Gabe caught sight of a man working his way through the village and hissed at Ezra, "Come inside 'fore they see us," and ducked into the tipi.

"What's wrong?" asked Ezra as he followed his friend.

"I don't want the traders to know we're in the village, I think it's best they don't know."

"Still suspicious, huh?"

They had just seated themselves when a scratch at the door followed by the voice of Cougar Woman, "Spirit Bear, there is someone here for you."

Gabe looked at Ezra, shook his head, "So much for hidin' out!" and rose to his feet, ducked through the door and was met by one of the traders.

The trader stepped back at the sight of Wolf, looked up at the men, "O, mon amie, I did not expect to see an English man! Nor one with a wolf! Is he safe?"

Gabe nodded, motioned for the man to be seated, then said in English, "I'm known as Spirit Bear, my friend," nodding to Ezra as he came from the tipi, "is Black Buffalo. My wife there is Cougar Woman, and his," nodding toward the women, "is Grey Dove."

"I am Gaston Durand of the Hudson Bay Company. We are here to trade with the *Nez Percé*. I did not know there were English with them. We have never seen any English traders with the *Nez Percé* before."

"Oh, we're not traders, we're just visitin'," explained Gabe. "We have a mutual acquaintance, you might say."

"Then if you are not traders, you must be trappers, so, if you have pelts or hides to trade, perhaps we could interest you to visit our blankets?"

Gabe glanced at Ezra, then back at Gaston, "No pelts, but do you have any coffee or sugar or cornmeal? We might be interested in them."

"Oui, we have some coffee and some sugar, but it is expensive. What do you have to trade?"

"Oh, we might come up with somethin'. How 'bout we visit you a bit later?"

"Good, good, then perhaps I will see you later!" declared Gaston, rising to leave. As he stood, Jean-Phillipe came to his side, glanced at Gabe and Ezra, frowning. Gaston saw his reaction and spoke to him in French, assuming the men did not understand and said to Jean-Phillipe, "These are English trappers with native women for their wives. I do not trust them, but they said they will trade with us." He turned back to Gabe and said, "Excuse me for using French, but Jean-Phillipe is not good with English." He turned back to his friend, saw him looking at the women and frowned, then motioned to Gabe and said in French, "This one is known as Spirit Bear," which brought a frown from Jean-Phillipe, "and this one," nodding to Ezra, "is Black Buffalo."

Jean-Phillipe extended his hand to shake with Gabe and Ezra, then said in stilted English, "Good meet you," nodding his head to each man as he shook their hands. They turned to leave and spoke to one another in low tones, making it impossible for Gabe or Ezra to hear or understand.

Ezra looked at Gabe, "I see what you mean. Although they didn't say anything wrong, it's just the way they acted, like they're up to somethin'. Did you see that other'n lookin' at our women?"

"Ummhumm, did you notice that Wolf didn't like 'em either? And one way or another, we're gonna find out what."

10 / BRUNO

"Is she . . .?" mumbled the mouse Henri. He looked up at Bruno, standing over the prone figure of a young woman, retying his sash around his middle. Blood showed on the knee of his greasy buckskins and he bent to grab some loose dirt to rub it away.

"What'chu think? Hehhehhe," giggled the big man, his broad grin showing through the matted whiskers, the gap between his tobacco stained tusks showed empty holes between the dark fangs. His eyes blazed with fury as his bulbous nose scrunched below his thick eyebrows that stood as tangled brush beneath his furrowed brow. "What she gets fer fightin' me. She won't be fightin' no more!" He dragged the bloody body with the stained and ripped buckskin tunic into the brush, then growled at his scrawny shadow, "C'mon, let's get outta here 'fore somebuddy comes!"

***

Little Owl wanted to talk with Cougar Woman and asked her to accompany her to check on the horses among the horse herd at the upper end of the village. As they walked, Little Owl asked, "Do you think I am too young to become a wife to Two Drums?" Little Owl was in a buckskin dress, a band of beads down each fringed arm and at the edge that hung below her knees, her sheathed knife hung between her shoulder blades, concealed under the dress. Cougar wore high topped moccasins with leggings under a long tunic, also fringed and beaded. Her beaded belt accented her trim waist and held the scabbarded knife at her back.

Cougar smiled as they walked, side by side, "Do you think you are too young?"

"I am not certain. I know of others that have taken a man at my age and some younger, but I never thought of being a wife. I have enjoyed our time of teaching and learning together and I would like to share what I know with others, but, if I am the mate of Two Drums . . ." she shrugged as she walked.

Cougar had come to think of Owl as her own daughter over the past months as they wintered in the cabin and could tell the girl was frustrated and confused. They walked a short way and Cougar asked, "How do you feel about Two Drums, in here" patting her chest, "I mean?"

Owl smiled, glanced at Cougar, "When I wake, he is who I look for first and when I go to sleep, I also want to see him to be certain he is there. When I am around him, I feel, well, warm and happy, but when he is not there, I always look for him to return soon."

Cougar also smiled, "I know he wants you to share what you know with his people and I know he feels the same way about you. His mother and her sister are happy for you and Two Drums and if you are happy, then you are not too young. You have learned many things with us, and you have shared with us what you know, it has been a good time for all. I think you will be happy together and we will see each other again."

"I would like that. You are like a mother to me and Spirit Bear has been like a father."

***

"Well, what have we here?" growled the slobbering Bruno, standing in the middle of the trail, arms folded across his chest and glaring at the two women.

Henri cackled and squeaked, "Looks like a couple plump chickens, ready to be plucked!"

The men looked past the women, seeing no one near and the trail bent around the point of the bluff, obscuring the village from view. Bruno grinned, "I think you're right! Think you can handle that little pullet while I see if this'n can take care of a real man!"

he growled, eyes blazing with lust and eagerness. He stretched out his meaty paws toward Cougar and she stepped back from the grimy mitts. Bruno leaned forward and Cougar grabbed his wrist, pulled him toward her and off balance, then kicked his feet from under him and she hit her elbow into his side as he fell face first into the dirt.

The big beast growled, rolled to his side to glare at the woman with surprise and hatred in his eyes. For a big man, he was amazingly agile and sprung to his feet. He dropped into a crouch, arms outstretched as he slobbered, "I'm gonna enjoy this! I'm gonna gut you after I use you and spread your innards over all these bushes for the buzzards and magpies."

Cougar had slipped her knife from the scabbard, but held it with the blade against her arm, hiding its presence from the monster before her. His flaring eyes gave away his charge and as he lunged, Cougar jumped high and to the side, slashing down on Bruno's arm as he stretched for her. The razor-sharp blade cut deep into his forearm, making the beast scream as he grabbed at his sleeve, startled at the blood.

"You cut me!" he slathered, "Ain't no woman ever cut me!" He looked at Cougar, down at the blood oozing between his fingers, then lifted his hand to see the deep cut, showing white of bone. "I'll rip you apart!" he screamed, dropping into a crouch, both arms outstretched.

***

The mouse had grabbed for Little Owl, but languages, customs and the ways of women were not all she had learned in the cabin. Owl pivoted on one foot, back-handing the little man across his face, then driving the knuckles of her fist into his ribs. As he bent over from the punch, she stepped to the side, hooked her heel behind his and thrust out with her hand on his face, driving him to his back. Before he could rise, she had her knife at his throat and her knee in his stomach, the other pinning down one arm. He reached for the knife with his free hand, but she swiped at his open palm, cutting it deep, then put the blade back at his throat, "Do not move or I will cut you so deep all your blood will wash this ground!" she growled, nose wrinkling, teeth showing and lip curling.

***

Bruno feinted his charge, making Cougar leap to the side, but he grabbed at her tunic and pulled. She spun, slashing out with the knife to cut his bicep, causing him to release his grip on her tunic. She slapped his arm to the side, stepped past him and spun, slashing at his hamstring. The knife cut deep and she jerked it across the massive muscle, thrusting it as deep as her strength allowed and the big man arched his back as he screamed, falling backwards to the ground, blood spurting and pooling.

The ruckus and screams had drawn others and a small crowd gathered to see the two voyageurs on the ground. Cougar looked at Little Owl, "Let him up."

Little Owl slowly lifted the knife, then quickly stood and stepped beside Cougar Woman. They looked at the crowd and saw Gabe pushing his way through. He stopped at the edge of the crowd, staring at the women and the men, Bruno still writhing and moaning on the ground, Henri trying to help his friend. Gabe quickly stepped before Cougar, "You alright?" Her arm with the knife hung at her side, the knife dripping blood.

She nodded, glared at the big man on the ground, "They attacked us."

Gabe grinned, "That was a mistake!" and reached his arms around Cougar and drew her close. He saw Little Owl replacing her knife in the sheath behind her back and reached out to bring her close, embracing the two together.

"What's goin' on?!" growled a man, pushing his way through the crowd. It was Gaston Durand and one glance showed Bruno and Henri together.

Henri squeaked, "Them women, they attacked us, for no reason!" shaking his finger at the two women in Gabe's arms.

Gaston looked at the blood pooling under Bruno's legs, "You better get some bandages and fix that! Now!" he barked at Henri.

He looked at the women, "You did that?" pointing to the big man and looking at Cougar.

Gabe stepped back, letting Cougar look at the questioner and she said, "Yes."

Gaston shook his head, looked up at Cougar, "You missed the most important part!"

She frowned, letting her expression tell her question.

"You shoulda made him a eunuch! That way he wouldn't bother any more women." He paused, looked back at Cougar, "Were you two coming up the trail?" pointing toward the horse herd, "and they were coming down?"

"Yes."

Gaston looked at Gabe, "Will you come with me, I'm afraid we might find somethin' else up that way."

Gabe frowned, looked at Cougar who nodded and then started up the trail with Gaston. As they walked, Gaston said, "Your woman done us all a favor. We told Bruno, the man she cut, if he ever touched another woman we would cut him ourselves. He just wouldn't listen."

They looked at the trail as they walked, saw the tracks of the two men, then the sign where there was scuffling and drag marks. Gaston walked to the brush, pushed them aside and saw the body of the woman left there by the two attackers. He shook his head, motioned to the brush for Gabe to have a look, then as they started back to the village, "This is bad," he mumbled as they neared the camp.

Adrien looked up to see the men coming, Gaston and Gabe supporting Bruno as he struggled, dragging one leg that was thoroughly bandaged by Henri. They stopped at the edge of the blanket, "I sent Henri for the horses, we need to pack up and leave." He spoke in French, hoping no one understood, "They left a dead woman in the brush back yonder," he said softly. "The woman of this man," nodding to Gabe, "did this to him when he and Henri tried to attack her and her daughter. He's lucky she didn't kill him."

Gabe was fluent in French and understood the conversation but did not let on he knew. Adrien looked at Gabe, back at Gaston. "Does anybody know?"

"Just him," nodding slightly toward Gabe.

Bruno was moaning and growling, getting weaker as the blood soaked the bandages. Gaston said, "He's gonna need sewing up, so I'll take 'em both back to camp. You might send him," nodding to Bernard Moreau, "to get Jean-Phillipe."

"Where's he at?" asked Adrien.

"Dunno, might need to look in every tipi."

Adrien shook his head, motioned for Bernard to fetch the other Lothario, then began gathering their goods together. He spoke to the waiting villagers in *Nez Percé*, "We will be back tomorrow!"

11 / RETRIBUTION

Gabe stepped away from the big man, dropping his arm to his side and making him shift his weight to Gaston. Both men looked at Gabe, frowning, until Gabe looked at Adrien. "This man is going nowhere! He and that little pipsqueak with him killed a woman and left her in the bushes back up the trail!" He spoke in English and sign, then repeated himself in the tongue of the *Nez Percé,* loud enough to be heard by the chief whose lodge was facing the compound where the traders had their blankets of wares.

The people nearby looked at one another and started talking, gesturing and two went to the lodge of Twisted Hair. The alarm had been sounded and within seconds, the group was surrounded by warriors, arrows nocked on the bows, some lifting lances. Twisted Hair came from his lodge, "What is this about a woman killed?"

Before he could answer, Adrien spoke to Gabe, "You are a white man and you turn against your own kind? Do you know what they will do?" he pleaded, speaking in stilted English.

"Not near enough! That filth also attacked my woman and our friend, he's lucky she didn't kill him, but if it had been some other woman, there would be another dead body in the brush!" spat Gabe, glaring at the leader of the Hudson Bay voyageurs. He looked at Twisted Hair as he came nearer and answered, "There is a woman in the brush, up the trail to the horse herd. This man, and the little one coming with the horses, did that."

With nothing more than a look, the warriors jerked the big man away from Gaston, dragging him to a framework used for smoking meat. As everyone watched, the warriors bound him to the frail frame, spread eagled, then stuffed leaves and grass in his mouth, gagging him. He struggled, pulling at the bonds, shaking his head side to side, wincing with pain, blood oozing down his leg and arms, but no one showed sympathy or mercy.

Adrien turned away, grabbing up the blankets loaded with their trade goods. Bernard Moreau, the long drink of water that worked the trades with Adrien, had voluntarily ran to fetch the horses, sending Henri Petit around the village and back to their camp. He worked quickly loading the pelts and parfleches onto the packhorses, stacking the rest of the trade goods in the panniers and tying them to the pack saddles. When Adrien handed off his armload, he kept his saddle horse, but sent the others away. He turned to face Gabe, "If you had kept quiet, we could have finished up and been on our way. That man," nodding toward the bound Bruno, "was wrong, but we need him. Losing him puts our entire mission in jeopardy! Why could you not mind your own business, she was just an Indian! Not like she was a real woman!"

"Keep talkin' and you'll probably end up on that rack with your friend," cautioned Gabe as he spat to the side, letting the leader of the voyageurs know what he thought of him. "That's the problem with those of your ilk, you think you're better than anybody that's different. That woman was more of a real human than bottom feeders like you and your bunch!"

Gabe looked up as Twisted Hair stepped closer, "The little one has gone!" declared the chief, "My warriors have gone after him."

Adrien Laurent heard the chief speak of Henri, then stepped toward the packs and Bernard, "Get out of here, now!" he hissed, motioning him away, "Tell the others they're comin' after the mouse!" While the chief was talking with Gabe and the others attention was on Bruno, Adrien slipped away, swung aboard his mount and disappeared into the trees and across the river, out of sight of the village.

Although the warriors knew of the camp of the traders, the exact location was unknown. While they searched for sign, Laurent and the others took the trail to the camp at a full gallop. They slid into their camp, shouting to the others, "Get those packs on those horses! We got Indians on our tail! *Se dépêcher!*" Everyone scurried around, gathering their gear, rigging the horses, while Gaston directed several to set up a defense of the camp.

***

Yellow Owl led the band of a dozen warriors. They picked up the trail within moments and started after the fleeing traders. They did not want the entire group, just the little one that was with the big man who attacked the woman. They did not know which one did the beating and killing of the woman, but the little one was there and must be returned to the village. Yellow Owl leaned low from his mount, looking at the tracks. It was obvious there were several horses, all running. He sat up, looked up the long draw and knowing the country, he turned to his men, "Bear Killer, you and four more, take that trail, come up on the timber from below." Bear Killer nodded, knowing exactly where Yellow Owl meant, motioned to the nearest four warriors and slapped legs to his mount to take the trail that led from the bottom of the long gulley.

Owl watched them leave, glanced at the sun then up the trail, wanting to give Killer and his men time to get into position. He motioned to his men to make ready, as several nocked arrows on their bows, holding two more arrows in the hand that gripped the bow. One warrior, Broken Lance, preferred the lance and tomahawk and fighting at close quarters, slipped his war shield on his forearm, nodding to Yellow Owl with one eyebrow cocked up and a grin tugging at one corner of his mouth. Owl nodded, then gigged his horse at a walk up the trail.

They followed the draw within a quarter mile of its origin at the crest of the butte, then Yellow Owl motioned to his followers and they rode up the bank to the flat-top away from the timber, dropped into the next draw that held several thickets of stunted juniper that would offer cover. From the crest, Owl spotted a thin spiral of smoke that marked the camp's location, probably due to the traders snuffing out the fire. He had hunted this area many times and knew it well. They tethered their horses and started the last hundred fifty yards on foot, scattering through the shrubs and trees as they approached.

All the Voyageurs were armed with rifles and at least two pistols each and Gaston had five of the men stationed along a breastwork of logs and brush, anxiously looking to the front for Indians and behind them to see if the others were ready to leave. The sudden blast of a rifle firing brought everyone's attention to the front, but the Nez Percé warriors were well concealed. The shooter, one of the younger ones that usually tended the horses, whined, "Je pensais en avoir vu un!" Another grumbled, "He didn't see anything, he's just scared."

The shooter stood for a better look and an arrow whispered through the air and impaled the man in the neck. He choked, gurgled, spat blood as he sunk to his knees and fell onto the breastwork.

"There they are!" screamed one man, lifting his rifle and firing. Suddenly shots rattled across the line, then mumbling and scrambling as they frantically worked at reloading the rifles. Gaston shouted, "Use your pistols!"

Yellow Owl screamed his war cry and signaled his men to attack. Arrows whipped through the air, a few finding flesh and eliciting screams from the victims. War cries of Owl's warriors shattered the stillness of the forest, birds flew from the trees, squirrels scolded then disappeared, an eagle lifted high on a current, screaming as he looked below. Scattered gunfire rattled through the trees, until the second band under Bear Killer screamed their war cries and charged through the trees.

The men with the horses grabbed their rifles and opened fire on the charging band that came from behind their camp, dropping two of the Nez Percé. Bear

Killer and the other two dropped into the brush and disappeared as quickly as they appeared. The gunfire from the other side had abated and the shooters scrambled back to the horses. The Voyageurs swung aboard the skittish horses and dug heels to the ribs of the mounts. The horses dug deep, kicking up clods of dirt as they lunged under their riders, anxious to leave the fight. One man lay low on his horse's neck, an arrow protruding from his shoulder and flopping with every clatter of hoof from his horse.

The Voyageurs followed Adrien as they ran from the trees, taking a deep cut from the butte top toward the valley below. It was the trail they rode from the river and was easily followed, twisting through the brush and trees that lined the dry creek bed. They kept to the fast pace, strung out as they were, each one anxiously looking behind them for any pursuit. When they broke from the mouth of the ravine, they were at the bank of the river, about five or six miles downriver from the village of the Nez Percé. Adrien called a stop and everyone slid from their mounts, letting the horses drink and graze as they buried their faces in the shallows of the river, drinking deeply themselves.

Adrien asked, "Lose any?"

"One of the young 'uns has an arrow we need to remove. One of the others didn't make it. But the mouse did and of course, Bruno didn't."

Adrien grumbled, "Réprouver!"

"Ummhmmm, he is a reprobate, no doubt about it. But he was strong and he'll be missed when it comes to hoisting those bundles of pelts!"

***

Yellow Owl led the warriors back into the village, two horses carrying the bodies of the slain. Gabe and Ezra heard the commotion and went near but stayed far enough away so as not to intrude, yet the bodies of the warriors caused a commotion among the villagers. The mothers and wives of the downed warriors wailed and wept, staggering to their lodges with others at their sides, helping the grieving women. Warriors gathered near the lodge of the chief, angry and demanding vengeance, shouting and screaming war cries and wails of anger and grief. The chief stood before them, arms raised and spoke rapidly and animatedly, motioning to the bound voyageur and to the lodges of the wailing women.

Gabe and Ezra could not make out what was said, but Gabe looked at Ezra, "I'm guessin' the Frenchies got away, but not without taking a toll on the Nez Percé."

"And I'm thinkin' we might not be too welcome here after all this," replied Ezra. The men turned away and started for the lodge, but were motioned close by Wind in her Hair, the mother of Two Drums.

"My son has told me of the attack on Little Owl and Cougar Woman. Are they alright?" she asked.

"Yes, they did more harm to the men that *tried* to attack them than was done to them," explained Gabe.

"My son thinks he should seek vengeance on the men that did this," offered Wind, posing it more as a question than a statement.

"The worst of the two has already been taken. He is bound at the rack in the compound and Twisted Hair will see to his punishment. I don't think Two Drums should be thinking about vengeance, but I understand how he feels. Have him come to our lodge when he returns, we'll talk to him."

She smiled, nodding, "I was hopeful you would speak with him."

12 / DEPARTURE

Gabe glanced up at Two Drums, "We'll be leavin' in the morning." They had been talking for a while with Gabe encouraging the young man to focus on his future with Little Owl instead of thinking about vengeance. Cougar Woman added, "She has already shown herself to be a warrior when she took him down and threatened to cut his throat!"

"She did not tell of that! She took him down?"

"Ummhmm, it happened very fast. When I looked, she already had him on his back with her knee in his stomach and the knife at his throat. You should remember that. She learned well," added Cougar, smiling mischievously at the young man.

Two Drums grinned, nodded, then frowned, "I thought you would stay," he started, but the bowed head of Gabe stopped him. He looked at the others, nodded, "Because of what happened with the traders?" he questioned.

"It's not a good time for strangers to be in the village. Your people are riled up, as they should be and not all of them are happy with us bein' here," suggested Ezra. "Sides, we was only bringin' you back to your people like we promised and now you'n Little Owl need to line out your plans and such."

"But where will you go?"

Ezra glanced at Gabe and nodded for him to speak up. With a grin, Gabe started, "We'll probably cross back over the Bitterroots, then go north. Lotta country to see and people to meet, we heard tell the Kutenai were good folks and some o' the others. The Coeur D'Alene and the Pend d'Oreille are said to be friendly too."

**

The heavy clouds were outlined in gold and the dark masses were tinged a muted pink. The sun was just making its presence known as it shot lances of gold above the low-lying clouds and Gabe and company smiled at the colors of the new day. Two Drums stood beside Little Owl, his mother and her sister near, as they bid their good-byes to their friends. Wind in her Hair spoke, "You will always be welcome in our lodge. You must return soon."

Cougar smiled down at the women, her hand

resting lightly on the shoulder of her son bound in the cradle board that hung from the pommel of her saddle. "Your son is a fine man and the woman he has chosen will be a good mate for him. They will have many children and you will be blessed with the laughter of young ones in your lodge." She paused and looked at Little Owl, the girl she thought of as a daughter, "Remember all you have learned and share it with others." Little Owl smiled, nodded, trying to keep the tears from falling and lifted her hand to wave to her friends as they rode from the village.

They took the trail that rode the foot of the slope at the tree line behind the village, it led around the point and to the river's edge. Ezra was leading with Dove close beside as they pushed the horses into the water to wade across the shallows onto the far sandbar.

"We're gonna go back the way we came, at least until the fork in the river. Twisted Hair said the trail that follows the north fork will take us into what he called Buffalo Flats. He said they go there in the fall to hunt buffalo," said Gabe as he and Cougar came up the bank, their horses stopping to shake the water free.

"Did he say how long it'd take us to get through the mountains?" asked Ezra, turning his bay to the trail.

"He said it takes his people all of a week, but we might do it in a little less. But there's plenty salmon in the river!"

"They do make good eatin'," answered Ezra.

It was an ancient trail they followed, hugging the north bank of the winding river. Most of the morning, they were in dry country with bald slopes above them, scrub timber across the river, but when the river made a wide bend around the point of a long ridge, the terrain changed to thicker timber and steep mountains. They nooned at the mouth of a feeder creek that came from low rising mountains to the north and spread a wide alluvial plain at the mouth of the wide cut. The spread was covered with tall grass, waving in the mild breeze that filtered down the canyon and the creek chuckled over rocks showing its whitewater that carried snowmelt runoff.

The women sat the cradleboards against a big log with a few branches still showing green and offering shade for the little ones. Chipmunk sat between his daddy's legs, content in his warmth. Gabe had climbed the shoulder of the hill beside their camp for his usual reconnoiter of the area, looking for game and any threat to their safety. He slipped and slid down the steep slope, watching the women tending the fire fixing their meal and Ezra busy with the little one. He smiled as he walked into camp, "You know, it's been quite a while since it's been just the four of us, an' the little ones of course. It's kinda nice, don't cha think?"

Cougar looked up at her man, offering him a cup of coffee, "Yes, but I miss the young ones. I enjoyed having them with us. It was like having our own village."

Gabe smiled as he looked around their camp, "We keep goin' like we are, we'll have our own village soon enough!"

Ezra chuckled, "Listen to him talk! We've got twice as many as you and you're already talkin' about a village!"

It was a pleasant time together as they sat around the low burning fire, enjoying their meal while the horses rested and grazed. They were not in a hurry and were uncertain where they were headed, but they were happy to be together and traveling in new country.

**

The blood had clotted and caked on the back of Bruno's leg and both arms. He hung limply at the smoke rack, his legs tired from standing and the one with the deep cut had given out. The camp was quiet and dark until a gruff looking lance carrying warrior accompanied a matronly grey-haired woman toward the bound man. Bruno stirred and stood, watching the two approach, not knowing what to expect with most of the camp turned in for the night. The woman sat a basket nearby and withdrew some poultices and soft buckskin bandages. She started with his left arm with the deep cut on the forearm. She wiped the blood off with a rag of trade cloth, then applied a poultice and tightly wrapped the bandage.

Bruno breathed deeply, his shoulders rising as he came full awake with the woman's work on his arm. He watched silently as she bandaged the upper right arm, then stood back to look at the deep gouge at the back of his leg. The blood flow had stopped with lumps of clots that held the cut trousers leg in the matted hair, cloth and blood. She looked up at him, muttered something to the warrior beside her. He grunted and nodded, and the old woman bent to her basket and brought out a long and semi-circular needle. Bruno's eyes flared as he looked at the needle and then to the woman. He knew his wound needed closing and the only way was for some sewing to be done, he slowly lifted his head, nodded and gritted his teeth, letting the woman go to her work.

The woman mumbled to the warrior as she worked, her manner telling of her contempt for the captive and her dislike for her work, but she continued. Bruno was certain she was intentionally being rough with him as she used split tendon to draw the meat of the wound together and tie it off. She roughly wiped the wound clean, having cut away a good portion of his britches to reveal the wound. Another poultice, more bandages and she was finished. She sat back, nodded and grunted as she looked up at the big man. She picked up her basket and started to turn away, then looked back at Bruno and without warning, kicked him in the crotch and stepped away, laughing and showing both her teeth in her wide and cackling mouth.

She motioned to the warrior and turned away, walking into the darkness laughing to return to her lodge. The warrior laughed, jammed the butt end of his lance into Bruno's stomach, laughed again and walked away. Bruno struggled for breath, shaking his head and mumbling curses as he tried to straighten up. As he pulled at the bonds on his wrists, pulling himself to his feet, he felt the one on his left give a little. He twisted to look and saw slack in the binding, then looked around at the quiet camp. No one was moving, the shadows of the night obscuring anything and anyone from his view, but it was quiet, even the dogs were asleep.

He began working at the loose bond in earnest, feeling it loosen with every tug. He pulled with all his available strength, somewhat lessened by the blood loss, but still considerable. As he pulled, he saw the upright on the smoke rack move, then looked to the other one and pulled both inward. They gave a little, creaking slightly, but still moving. He worked, pulling and wiggling, until the one on his left began to crack, then he applied all his force to that one, pulling it downwards. Within moments, it gave, a bit of a creak emitting as the green pole bent, then a crack and it gave way.

Bruno stood still, holding his arm out as if still secure and looked throughout the camp, but nothing stirred. He continued to work at it and in a short while, both arms were free and he bent down to undo the binding at his ankles. He was tussling with the rawhide straps when something cold touched his neck and he jerked back to see a skinny mongrel wagging his tail and looking up at the big man. Bruno looked around, saw no one, bent to pet the dog and whisper to him, then finished freeing his ankles.

Staying in the shadows and moving silently on moccasined feet, he trotted away from the camp toward the horse herd. He knew there would be guards, probably young bucks, but he needed a horse. Moving silently from rock to brush to anything that would hide his presence, he spotted the nearest guard, a young man, dozing against a big boulder. Bruno crept near, then grabbed the young man before he woke and twisted his head like the stem of an apple, breaking his neck, then dropped the dead body at his feet. He saw the guard had a bow and arrows, but they were useless to the big man because every time he tried to use a bow, he would draw it so far the bow would splinter and break, but he grabbed the knife and scabbard from the guard's belt and jammed it behind his sash.

With a rawhide rope in hand, he slowly worked

his way through the horse herd, speaking softly as he moved at a crouch, keeping his head below the backs of the horses. He spotted a big grey that did not shy away from him and quickly slipped the rope over his neck. He fashioned a twisted halter, swung aboard the horse and lying low on its neck, he pushed his way toward the trees. Within moments he was in the timber and moving away from the village. He remembered Adrien and Gaston talking about returning downstream on the Clearwater and decided to try to catch up with the other voyageurs, even though they left him behind and did nothing to free him, they would be his best chance for escaping the Nez Percé.

The first grey light of early morning showed the ripples in the water of the fast-flowing river beside the trail. Bruno had been away from the village at least an hour, maybe two, when he spotted the camp of the voyageurs, already buzzing with activity as they were readying to leave. Bruno hailed them with, *"Bonjour le camp!"*

Two men jumped, rifles in hand, as they stepped to the edge of the camp facing the unexpected man on horseback. Bruno lifted his hand high, said, *"C'est moi, Bruno!"*

He heard the ruckus as the guard shouted to the interior of the camp, telling about Bruno's arrival. As he rode into the camp, Adrien stepped forward, "How'd you get away?"

"I tore myself free, broke the rack an' left!" he explained, simply.

"Anyone following you?" asked Gaston, looking past the big man into the dim light in the valley.

"None that I saw. No one knew I broke loose!"

"They will soon enough, then they'll be hot on your trail that leads right to our camp," grumbled Adrien, looking at the big man, glancing at his wounds and saw they were bandaged. He pointed with his chin, "They do that? The bandages?"

"Yeah, an old woman did it last night. Even sewed me up," motioning with a head bob to his leg. "I think they just wanted me to live longer so they could torture me more." He took a deep breath, "That ol' woman, after she sewed me up and bandaged me an' all, she turned back and kicked me in the crotch! Laughed about it too!" The men that had gathered near laughed as he told about it, but he growled at them, his usual disagreeable self and they backed away.

Gaston looked at Adrien, "So, now what? They'll be after us sure, now. We gonna go downriver?" nodding to the trail that followed the river.

"No, I don't think so. When we started this trip, we were gonna head east out of here, go to the Flatheads and Kootenai, then back around to the west. I think we'll do just that. We can take that cut yonder," nodding to the break in the hills east of the river, "and join up with the old trail that follows the Lochsa into

Flathead country. But we need to make 'em think we're goin' downriver here, so have a couple men trail some pack horses a ways then cut over the hills and join up. Make sure they hide their trail as best they can, anything to confuse them Nez Percé."

Gaston shook his head, believing the plan to be a foolish one, but he went to find the men that would try to fool the warriors that would be on their trail. He believed they would be nothing more than sacrificial offerings to appease their pursuers, but there was a slim chance they might escape, so, who to choose?

13 / LOCHSA

It was a good trail. Traveled by Nez Percé, Palus, Cayuse, Coeur D'Alene and many other ancient peoples from the west for eons, migrating east to the land of the bison. And Sélis, Pend d'Oreille, even Blackfoot that went west into the canyon with the river ripe with salmon, all traveling on the same trail, leaving cairns to mark the way.

Mid-morning they passed the confluence with the Selway river that held the trail they followed when they brought Two Drums and Little Owl to the Nez Percé. Gabe looked around, "Those are some mighty big trees," nodding to a mountain side populated with the towering red cedar. "Course, most of the trees, even the ones that we've seen in other parts of the Rockies, are bigger. Must be the climate, which is a little wetter'n what we're used to!" For most of the trail, the couples rode two abreast. When the natives traveled to the east to the flatlands that held the massive herds of bison, they would carry their hide lodges on travois and haul the meat back to their villages on the carriers. The numbers of travelers and horses pulling travois naturally widened the trail over the years, benefitting Gabe and company.

Just before their stop for the mid-day meal and rest for the horses, they jumped a bunch of big horn sheep that were at river's edge. Several of the rams had full curl horns and stood watch as the ewes pushed the lambs up the steep hillside to make their escape. With one last look at the intruders, the rams took to the precipice, finding footholds where there were but narrow cracks on the rocky face, bounding up the steep wall as if they were just out for a morning walk. Gabe nodded to the fleeing sheep, "Don't you wish you could climb cliffs like that?" speaking over his shoulder to Ezra.

"Nope! Don't like heights! You know that! I'm quite content right here on the back of my horse. Don't have no hankerin' at all to get up there an' fall off. Uhnuh," stated Ezra.

"If you could climb like they do, you wouldn't be afraid of heights," suggested Gabe.

"I ain't afraid! I'm just smart enough to know God didn't make those cliffs for man, otherwise we'd have pointy hoofs instead of feet. So, if God didn't make 'em for us, why climb on 'em?"

Gabe chuckled at the logic of his friend as he looked around at the heavily timbered mountains. They had passed several ravines where an alluvial plane had been pushed into the edge of the river, then sprouted in trees and brush, but the flat of the plane also altered the course of the river, pushing it to bend around to make its way down the canyon. It was just such a flat that beckoned for the travelers to take their mid-day break.

When the sun nestled in the mouth of the canyon, the timbered mountains to the north and south appeared as dark hands holding the golden orb and the brightness lengthened the shadows before them, Gabe and company found another flat at the bend of the river to make their camp. A narrow stream fell from the ravine on the north bank, chuckling its way over the rocks and splashing to a pool below, then crossed the trail before trickling into the wide river to be carried away. The sky was clear and they saw no need for lean-to shelters, preferring the canopy of stars for their nights blanket and once the horses were tended, Gabe climbed the hill, Wolf at his side, cased scope in one hand and rifle in the other for his customary reconnoiter.

While the women fed the babies, Ezra took Chipmunk with him to fetch some firewood. With the youngster carrying a stick almost as big as he was and Ezra with an armful, they marched back into camp and dropped their loads, smacked their hands together and sat down, the toddler mimicking his father in every move. The women laughed, enjoying the sight and seeing the little one wanting to be just like his daddy.

The women had the meal almost ready when Gabe came from the hilltop, following Wolf bounding into camp. Gabe looked around, smiling at the familial scene, then turning his back on the women, spoke to Ezra, "You might wanna get your rifle handy."

Ezra's eyes flared as he stood and went to the stack of gear to fetch his rifle, followed by Gabe who ambled behind, trying not to show any concern. Ezra looked at his friend, "So, what's goin' on?"

"Prob'ly nothin', but I did see a mama grizzly escortin' her two cubs and comin' down the trail, big as you please. We might need to discourage her if she decides to visit us for supper. She'll prob'ly smell the cookin' and want to come for a sample."

"I hate it when company comes without an invitation! You didn't invite her, did'ju?"

"Nope, not a'tall," chuckled Gabe, shaking his head slightly.

Both men naturally checked the loads and priming in their rifles, then the pistols in their belts and satisfied, went back to the log by the fire. The horses were all tethered between the fire and the river, enjoying the tall grass at river's edge and if the bear was to leave the trail, she would have to come through the trees and meet the men first. The women noticed the men's actions and Cougar Woman asked, "Visitors?"

"One of the locals, got a couple little ones with her. I'm thinkin' she'll take to the tall and uncut 'fore trying to come to supper," explained Gabe.

***

Henri Petit, the mousy one, wasn't good for much, being so little and all, but he was the best tracker in the bunch. It was the one time he was a valued member of the group and he relished the respect and attention gained at such times. He had dropped to one knee, reaching down to touch and examine the tracks that covered the trail before them. He glanced ahead, then back at the tracks, stood and turned to face Adrien, "Looks like six or seven, traveling easy, no hurry. Maybe a family or a hunting party."

"Can you tell if they're natives or others?" asked Gaston.

"Nah, there's nothing distinct about any of 'em. All seem to be carryin' a load, whether people or packs, dunno."

"How far ahead?" asked Adrien.

"At least a day, thereabouts," answered the squeaky one.

Adrien looked at Gaston then back at Henri, "Alright, let's keep going, need to find a place to camp before it gets too dark."

Henri stepped back aboard his horse, started to rein around to fall back in the line of voyageurs until Adrien ordered, "You stay out front, watch the sign and maybe you can find out a little more about them. Scout out ahead far enough to warn us if necessary."

Henri looked at Adrien, suspecting the man had other ideas but he was a little lacking in intelligence and let the thought drop. But he also knew the scout was also the most exposed and likely to fall prey of any attack, be it man or beast and that was something he did understand. The little man was watchful of his surroundings and anxious to find a campsite. His horse suddenly spooked and Henri grabbed at the pommel and pulled tight on the reins, clutching at the saddle leather and the ribs of the horse with his legs. The horse dropped his head between his hooves, driving his front legs into the dirt and stretched out, kicking at the treetops with his hind feet. Henri's hat flew off and he tried to grab at it as it left his head. But his mistake at reaching for the hat and letting go of the pommel, unseated him as his rump lifted at least a foot off the saddle. Then the horse reared, catching the little man in the saddle, and pawed at the sky with his forefeet, whinnying and snorting, then stabbed at the ground again, his nose between his feet. He twisted his body, kicking at the clouds, then lifted off the ground and sun-fished, dropping his rider from the saddle to crash into the dust at the edge of the trail. Free of his burden, the horse went bucking up the trail, stirrups, reins, tail and mane flying and everything else flopping as if waving goodbye to the man in the dirt.

Henri shook his head, pushing his face out of the dirt, rose to his hands and knees, spitting rocks and wiping dirt from his eyes. He sat back on his haunches, looking around to get his bearings, and saw nothing but dirt and trees. Everything was silent until a circling osprey chirped and scolded the man in the dirt then flew away to its nest, somewhere high in the treetops.

Henri stood, dusting himself off and stepped close to the tracks left by his spooked horse, saw the deep hoofprints where the animal had stabbed at the dirt, then lifted his eyes up the trail, hoping to see the animal returning. But he was disappointed. He looked around, trying to determine what had spooked the horse, saw nothing but a dry twisted branch. He picked it up, looked at it and guessed the horse must have thought it was a snake. As he tossed it aside, an awful stench filled his nostrils, but a sudden chattering and hissing scared him as he looked toward the riverbank. The whites of his eyes showed as he stuttered, backing away from multi-hued brown and black creature. With a small flat head that hung low, long teeth that showed as his nose wrinkled and he hissed, the creature slowly approached Henri. Long claws showed at each foot, its head swung side to side. Henri slapped at his sash, feeling for his pistol, but touched only the hilt of his scabbarded knife.

Henri shouted at the low-slung beast, waving his arms trying to frighten it away, but the wolverine did not give ground. Henri knew this animal as a skunk bear and knew it was pound for pound the most ferocious creature in the mountains. The little Frenchman was breathing heavy, feeling his way back with each step, not knowing what was behind him. A quick glance behind the creature saw the remains of a partially eaten and long-dead mountain sheep. Henri slipped the knife from the scabbard when a rifle roared, echoing back and forth in the narrow canyon. A puff of dust rose from the left flank of the wolverine, making the animal stumble and spin around, biting at its own rear. The beady eyes saw others coming and it took off to the trees, limping slightly, but moving as fast as a charging bear.

Henri looked up to see Gaston, a rifle at his shoulder with a thin tendril of smoke lifting from the barrel. He lowered the weapon and came to the side of Henri. He looked down at the man, "Where's your horse?"

"He spooked, bucked me off, and took off up the trail. I didn't know what spooked him till that thing come outta the brush!" nodding to where the wolverine disappeared. "I lost my pistol and my rifle is still in the scabbard on that horse!" he nodded to the bend in the trail.

Gaston looked around, saw a large sandbar that pushed into the river and held considerable grass and some willows at the lower end. "We'll camp here tonight. You better start hoofin' it to catch that horse before it gets too dark!"

"Lemme use your horse to go get him," pleaded Henri, his hand outstretched.

"Nope. You lost him; you go find him. And I suggest you get a move on before Adrien gets here."

Henri stubbed his foot in the dirt, looked at Gaston, then started up the trail for his horse.

14 / SIGHTING

They heard the huffing of the mama bear first. Then all the sounds of the forest ceased, no birds sang, no squirrels chattered and it seemed as if even the wind stopped. Then the low voice of Gabe hissed, "There!" as he lifted the muzzle of his rifle to point. A tree shaking roar split the quiet, drowning out the rippling of the river and the creaking of the dead snags in the woods. The big bear was standing, cocking her head to the side, the massive mouth open and showing long teeth as the roar resounded and echoed across the canyon. She snapped her jaws and slapped at a tree branch in front of her, huffed a few times, then opened up and let another roar fill the wide canyon, the trees doing little to muffle the sound.

Gabe and Ezra came to their feet, rifles at their shoulders but the muzzles toward the ground, standing feet apart and braced for both the recoil of the rifles and the attack of the bear. Wolf was beside Gabe, standing in his attack stance, head lowered, eyes glaring, teeth showing, but Gabe spoke softly, "Stay boy."

Neither man would move from their mark, standing before their families, ready to defend to the death. But the roar of a grizzly can strike fear into any living being and they felt as well as heard the roar of the big bear. The women had their rifles propped on the log before them and Dove was on one knee, holding Chipmunk tightly, glancing to the baby in the cradleboard. Cougar had leaned the cradleboard with Bobcat against the log and had one hand on the board and the other on her rifle. Gabe heard the horses moving about, undoubtedly smelling and hearing the beast and a little fearful of an attack.

The two bear cubs scampered up the big red cedar beside their mother and seated themselves side by side on a big branch, both reaching to the trunk for stability as they looked down on their mother.

Gabe said, "She ain't gonna leave till her cubs come down. Everybody stay still and don't look directly at her," speaking softly. The men stood stoically, unmoving, watching the biggest beast of the woods, waiting for her to move and hoping she would move away.

The big bear looked up at her cubs, barked and snapped her jaws at them, then watched as they tenuously worked their way back down the towering tree. The cubs disappeared behind the thick brush, then the mama bear dropped to all fours. Gabe was holding his breath, waiting for her to either attack or disappear, then he heard her huffing fade as she scooted her youngsters away, across the trail and into the woods.

Gabe sucked in a deep breath, saw Ezra do the same and they turned to see the women, both standing with rifles in their hands and Chipmunk sitting on the log before them. Everyone smiled and laughed at the others and lowered the rifles, standing them at the log, then dropped to the log themselves. Gabe reached for a cup and the pot to pour himself some coffee but had three others thrust before him that he had to fill first. As they all sat back and sipped the coffee, Ezra was the first to speak. "Guess she realized this party was by invitation only and she didn't have one!"

"That's probably what she was so upset about!" declared Gabe, chuckling, running his free hand through the scruff of Wolf's neck.

"Well, the next time, she won't get an invitation either!" stated Dove, laughing at the men.

"She probably saw us as the intruders, she didn't give *us* an invitation," suggested Cougar, as she poured the coffee.

***

For most of the next day, the canyon walls seemed to push in on the travelers, with butte faces almost perpendicular as they rose from the river, scattered greenery clinging to the steep slopes. The trail they followed appeared to hang suspended over the rushing waters of the river, narrowing as they rounded the points of razor-edged hogbacks. But although they were dropping from the higher elevations, the trail was easy and the animals had little difficulty. By mid-afternoon, the buttes retreated, laying back from the river, letting the shadows give way to sunshine. But the reprieve was short-lived and the walls pushed in again and the river snaked its way ever westward. As the sun dropped behind the hilltops on the west, the valley opened again, revealing sparsely vegetated hillsides and dry country.

The second day after their interlude with the mama grizz, they were still on the trail that shadowed the river, but the hills gave way offering a little more elbow room to the group. When dusk fell, they were at the fork of the river and the trail stayed with the shallow stream that came from the north. They made camp and as the men were watering the animals, Gabe said, "The hair on my neck has been prickling all day. I ain't seen nothin' but, somethin's makin' me a mite uncomfortable."

"Ummhmm, me too. But shore don't know what it is," answered Ezra, looking upstream of the gurgling creek. Crystal clear water splashed over the rocks, showing white water as it tumbled below. They were beside a deep pool below the cascades where brook trout were breaking the surface after mayflies and more.

"I'm climbin' that ridge yonder. Maybe it'll give me a better view of our back trail and more. Tell Cougar it might take a while, but Wolf's with me," directed Gabe. He turned back toward the camp, but the grassy flats for the horses' graze was closer and he picketed the horses. With scope and rifle in hand, he and Wolf crossed the trail and angled through the trees to zigzag their way to the top of the ridge. The crest of the ridge was about fifteen hundred feet above the valley floor and topped with solid rock. Gabe sat, legs drawn up, and placed his elbows on his knees with scope in hand as he began his reconnoiter. He moved the scope to follow the creek upstream as it carved its way alongside the trail. But both trail and creek bent around a butte, turning back to the east and out of sight.

Determined to see further, he rose and walked back along the ridge until he could see around the bend. He dropped to his haunches and stretched out the scope. The only living thing he saw was a big bull moose, standing in the middle of the creek, enjoying an evening snack of greenery, some hanging from his jowls. Gabe chuckled and rose to return to his first promontory.

He knew he would be sky lined, so he bellied down and stretched out. Something had raised his hackles and he always paid attention to his hunches and anything that would be a premonition of whatever sort, for many had been the time that paying attention paid off. He moved the scope slowly, looking for movement or anything out of the ordinary. There was one point on the back trail that disappeared behind a timber covered knob, but his elevation gave him a good view of the trail further back. He carefully and slowly scanned every stretch, remembering the trail from their travels in the afternoon. There were other stretches that were hidden behind ridges and buttes, but he watched, waiting, considering every possibility. He started to bring the scope closer, but something stopped him. He was taking shallow breaths, not wanting to move and then he saw it. A thin trail of smoke, that little waft of light grey smoke when the campfire first blazes up and ignites the sap and bark. Then the smoke feathered out and disappeared, probably filtered through the pine boughs overhead. But there had been fire and fire meant people and a mistake like that would mean those were not natives.

He kept the scope on the spot, moving it along the tree line and the river bank. Movement again, horses at the river's edge. He instinctively knew who they were, for there had been no other non-native people in the area. Those were the French Voyageurs from the Hudson Bay company. *But why would they be following us?* Gabe asked himself. He shook his head as he rolled to his side, looked at Wolf and asked, "So, Wolf, what do you suppose they're doing?"

Gabe crawled from the ridge top, stood and started back down the slope. Thinking all the while as to the why's of the followers. He slipped and slid, gravel and dirt giving way as he dug his heels in and made his way to the bottom.

As he walked into the camp, Ezra saw his expression and asked, "What is it?"

Gabe glanced up, lay his rifle against the log and lay the scope and case beside it, then looked up as Cougar handed him a cup of coffee. "It's those men from Hudson's Bay company. They're about a day, maybe less, behind us."

Ezra frowned, "I thought they were goin' back down the Clearwater river, back to the Snake."

"That's what I thought too, but they're behind us now."

"Maybe they go to trade with the Salish," offered Cougar Woman, dishing up a plate of stew for Gabe.

"Yeah, I thought that. If they are, they could go north like we talked about, trade with the Kutenai and others, then go back west to the post they came from. Which one was it? They called it the Buckingham House, didn't they?"

"That's what the one that saw us at the lodge said, but there's also posts north east, up Canada way," responded Ezra.

Gabe took a couple scoops of stew, thinking about the followers, then said, "I think we'd do well to put some distance between us."

"You mean travel at night?" asked Ezra.

Gabe nodded his head, "Right. We don't know if they're followin' us or just changing their trade route, but just the same, I'd feel better if we weren't crowded in a canyon like this," he said as he lifted his eyes to the nearby hills.

"Well, we certainly have the moon for it!" said Cougar Woman. "It's waxing full and we'll have a few nights with it full. That will put us out of the mountains and into Salish country."

"I like the sound of that," added Dove, glancing to the little ones, lying on the blanket beside her.

***

They finished their supper and were back on the trail as the fading light of dusk blended with the rising moon that was waxing full. Dim shadows painted a kaleidoscopic pattern across the trail and the forest was silent as the nocturnal creatures were slow in rousing for their night time rendezvous. The trail held to the west bank as they moved with the moon over their right shoulder, still resting on the jagged horizon of the shadowy mountains. Gabe noticed the trail was climbing, although the hills on either side faded. When he commented about it to Ezra, who rode beside him, Ezra said, "Prob'ly coz we're climbing an' they aren't!"

Gabe looked around in the light of the moon and stars, then to Ezra, "You might be right about that. Twisted Hair said this trail climbed over an easy pass. He said the trail intersects with the Nez Percé trail. I think he called it by the Salish name, *Naptnisaqs.* He said his people use that trail if they're camped further north, usually when they come this way for buffalo on the fall hunt."

"But this will take us onto the flats?" asked Ezra.

"Yeah, at least that's what Twisted Hair said."

With a short stop after about six miles, they crossed the creek to follow the trail that cut through the timber on the east side of the river, hugging the steep hillside in the thick timber. Wolf led the way in the dim moonlight, trotting easily on the wide trail, made so by eons of travelers making their way to the buffalo hunting grounds.

At the crest of the pass, the mountains opened wide, sharing the light of the moon and the clear night sky bedecked with millions of stars. The milky-way painted its broad highway to the afterlife, as many plains tribes believed and offered light for the way.

The air was cool, but clear, until Gabe reined up beside Wolf, who stood staring down the winding trail that disappeared in the darkness. One foot lifted, head erect, ears pricked forward and eyes blazing orange, the Wolf let a low growl rumble as he stared.

"What is it boy?" softly asked Gabe. Then he recognized the smell of elk, moments later heard the clatter of hooves moving through the downed timber, crashing their way through the thick pines. "Somethin' spooked 'em!" declared Gabe, glancing to Ezra.

"Could be 'nother Grizz!" suggested Ezra.

They sat quiet, waiting, listening, barely breathing. Ezra lifted his head, sniffing the air. A grizzly or any bear has a distinct and usually strong and unpleasant odor. Anyone experienced in the mountains could easily discern the smell of bear, elk and many other creatures of the woods. But nothing came, no other sound was made and Gabe gigged Ebony forward, waving Wolf to take the lead.

15 / QL'ISPÉ

The big black wolf trotted away, moving warily but quickly, obviously on the hunt. Gabe and the others followed close behind as the trail dropped from the crest of the pass. A narrow creek trickled alongside the trail, its headwaters just below the crest from a small spring fed pool. The path dropped from the higher reaches of the mountains, making its way alongside the fast falling creek that splashed over cascades like one continuous waterfall. It was soon fed by other mountain side run-off creeks and began to swell in size, yet still no wider than a horse could easily cross with one jump. The noisy creek often ducked under overhanging willows and oak brush, but continually wound its way along its ages old course.

Gabe and Ezra searched the trees on either side, scanning any open hillsides, looking for whatever had spooked the elk. But the moonlight showed nothing moving, other than the usual creatures of the night. In the distance a pair of coyotes yipped at one another, probably bragging about their day's kill. Nighthawks screamed from on high, cicadas chattered and an occasional owl asked his eternal question. Wolf had stopped in the middle of the trail when the unmistakable howl of a wolf lifted above the treetops. He stretched out and answered the forlorn howl, letting the lonesome she-wolf know he was near and interested. But no answer came and Wolf dropped his head and trotted on down the trail.

They had come most of three miles from the crest when the trail bent around the shoulder of a timber covered mound and the creek dropped over a waterfall. Wolf stopped in the trail, head lowered and eye blazing. Gabe stopped beside the Wolf, stared into the dark shadows beside the trail and saw movement. He slipped the Ferguson rifle from the scabbard, bringing it to full cock as he dropped it into the crook of his arm. He motioned the others to wait and gigged Ebony forward, but at the edge of the darkness, he swung down, and started forward. He called out softly, "If you can hear me, I mean you no harm." He repeated himself in Salish, believing they had passed out of the land of the Nez Percé and were now in the land of the Flathead.

He heard a moan, some scratching in the dirt, another low moan then nothing. Gabe paused, then cat footed forward, rifle held before him and letting his eyes become accustomed to the darker shadows. Another moan, and he saw a slight movement on the ground before him. He slowly stepped forward, dropped to one knee, and saw a man, a native, with dark splotches on his back, probably blood.

"I will help you, I am Spirit Bear, a friend," said Gabe, in Salish. The man stirred, moaned, but said nothing coherent. Gabe stood, staring into the dark, looking for any others, but saw nor heard nothing. He turned to call out, "Ezra, got a hurt man here. We need to help him. Bring the horses and come on."

Within moments the others were near and Ezra stepped down to help Gabe as Gabe instructed, "Let's get him out of these trees down the trail where there's more light." He looked back at Cougar Woman, "Bring the horses, we'll help this man into the light."

The two men, one on either side, helped the wounded man up and out of the trees, about twenty yards, then lay him on the slight slope beside the trail. Cougar Woman came to them, a parfleche of her bandages and remedies in her hand. Ezra fetched some wet rags, handing them off to Cougar Woman as she began cleaning the wounds and tending the wounded man. She spoke to him in Salish, and the man struggled to reply. "Blackfoot . . . attacked my family; we were at the hot springs when they came." He winced in pain, fighting for air and wanting to tell,

"I had gone to the trees before they came." He sucked in another breath; his face contorted as he struggled. "I think they killed my family."

He tried to twist around to see what Cougar Woman was doing, but she put a hand on his back. "Lie still, I have to take out these arrows."

He fought to speak, determined someone would know what happened. "I ran, but they shot me . . ." he groaned, doubling his fists as he fought. "I fell down the hill. I thought they would come after me, but they left." He paused, his breath coming sporadically, "I came to the trail, wanted to go back . . ." and he lapsed into unconsciousness.

Gabe had stood beside Cougar and heard the man's story, watched as Cougar finished cleaning the wounds and begin cutting to remove the broken off arrows still embedded in the man's back. He had taken three arrows, all were broken off near the entry point and had lost a lot of blood, but he fought to stay alive and Cougar thought he would live.

"It's gonna be light soon, I think we can make it to the hot springs and maybe take care of his family," suggested Gabe. He looked at Ezra, "How 'bout you ridin' down, have a look around, then we'll all go and camp where ever you say."

Ezra slowly nodded, "You gonna hold that fella on?" looking at the wounded man.

"Ummhmm, Chipmunk can ride with Dove that

little ways, you take Wolf."

Ezra nodded, checked the load in his rifle then swung aboard, called to Wolf and started on the trail. The path bore to the northeast and the first light of dawn showed itself on his right shoulder as he approached the hot springs. Steam plumes rose like whispers in the dim light, the massive boulders behind the springs stood like shrouded ogres behind the wispy plumes. Then the first ray of sunshine bent across the hilltops and illumined the mysterious grotto, revealing the bodies strewn about. The smell of blood and death were upon the place and carrion eaters had already begun their battle with one another. A badger was in a standoff with a coyote, while buzzards, ravens and magpies tussled over tidbits. Any living person that had been here was long gone, surrendering the fetid feast to the scavengers.

Ezra spotted a rockslide on the face of the opposing hill, a small meadow at its base and the stream close at hand. Judging it to be far enough away from the carnage to be safe and upwind, he chose that for the campsite. He waved the others over and began gathering some firewood for the ladies. As Gabe started tending the horses, Ezra came to his side, "We need to take care of some bodies over there," nodding toward the boulders and the hot springs. "Looks like four or five, as the man said."

The women had the man prostrate on the blankets

near the fire and Cougar was checking his bandages. Gabe saw the man's chest rise and fall and glanced at Cougar, a question on his expression. She looked up at her man, nodded, then stood to help Dove prepare the meal. Ezra had the one short handled shovel they always carried and motioned for Gabe to follow.

The hot springs had a slight mineral odor, but the deep pool of clear aquamarine water steamed and billowed the misty cloud above. They picked a spot beside the massive boulders and while Ezra started digging, Gabe fetched the bodies. All had been mutilated almost beyond recognition as human and the carrion eaters were reluctant to leave, but Gabe hastened them on their way. He rolled the bodies onto a blanket found with the scattered belongings and dragged them to the burial site. As near as he could make out there was an older man and woman, a girl of about fifteen summers and a boy of maybe twelve. Their clothing was nothing more than strips of buckskin, tattered pieces torn at by the coyotes and buzzards and the men decided to make a common grave.

"He said it was his family. I'm thinking maybe his mother and father, a sister and a brother. I thought we'd find a younger woman, his wife maybe, and a couple youngsters." He glanced at Ezra, "How old do you think he is?" pointing with his chin back toward the camp.

"Oh, I'd say maybe twenty, give or take a couple years."

"Yeah, probably." He thought a bit while Ezra filled in the grave, then added, "Didn't see any sign of any Blackfoot, no blood or nothin', so I reckon the attack took 'em by surprise and they didn't get to fight back. Tough."

Ezra flipped the shovel to Gabe to finish the job as he climbed out of the shallow hole and found a seat on a big rock. Gabe grabbed the shovel and went to work as Ezra watched.

"So, you think this'ns a Salish?" asked Ezra.

"No, Cougar says those big shell earrings are what the *Ql'ispé* or Kalispel wear. She said the Frenchies were callin' 'em Pend d'Oreille. She said they're related to the Salish and the language is pretty much the same."

"Any idea as to how far his village might be?" asked Ezra.

"Not yet, but we can't hang around here too long. We traveled all night to get away from the Voyageurs and I still don't want to have to deal with them. Even though that big 'un was in the hands of the Nez Percé, the rest of 'em weren't too happy we told Twisted Hair about what happened with the woman."

The sun was above the mountains, the warmth of the light on their backs comforting as they finished with the grave. They had packed several hat sized rocks from thereabouts to cover the grave and discourage the scavengers. They stood with hats in hand, said a brief prayer over the grave, and started back to camp.

As they sat about enjoying the breakfast of thin strips of venison fried with camas roots and sided by cornmeal biscuits, Gabe asked, "Think he'll be able to travel soon?"

"How soon?" asked Cougar Woman.

"Well, I figger we can rest the horses and ourselves until 'bout noon," he glanced at the sky as he spoke, "but we need to keep movin' what with those Voyageurs on our trail."

"If he comes around and his bleeding stops, he might ride with some help."

"Reckon we'll just have to see how he's doin' when it's time to go, then," suggested Ezra.

Gabe nodded, took another bite then added, "Ummhmm, and we'll head north as soon as we get outta these mountains," looking around as he spoke. "Cougar says the Kalispel are to the north or northwest."

16 / DISCOVERY

Henri Petit was still scouting for the Voyageurs, staying about two miles ahead and locating their campsites for each stop. He had lost interest in the tracks of those that traveled the same route before them, believing they were nothing more than a native family bound for the buffalo hunting grounds. They had been on the trail for several days and were pushing the horses as much as they could, determined to make it to the villages of the Salish, Coeur D'Alene and more before returning to their trade post with the bounty. This was to be a profitable trip for each man, sharing in the take equally when the pelts were exchanged at the post. He was day dreaming about what he would do with his biggest payday ever, when the trail left the bank of the river and bent to the north, to follow a narrow creek.

He paused at the fork in the valley, one carrying the Lochsa river to the east, the other with the well-traveled trail they chose to follow to the flats and the land of the Salish and more. Then he saw sign of a previous camp and his curiosity tugged at him as he pushed his mount off the trail to examine the sign. The skilled tracker wasted little time checking the tracks of those that had camped here no more than the night before. He saw the indentations where two cradleboards were propped, the tiny moccasined tracks of a toddler, the small moccasins of what he was certain were women. Their tracks were near the cradleboards and the toddler and closer to the firepit. They had knelt before the fire and the knee imprints showed they wore tunics or dresses. Larger footprints showed two men were also a part of the camp. He stood, thinking he had discovered nothing new, until a different print caught his eye. He dropped to one knee, reaching out to examine the prints of a wolf, almost the size of his entire hand. *That's a big wolf!* he thought as he looked around. It would not be unusual for a wolf to enter the camp after it had been abandoned, looking for scraps and more. But then he saw the prints of the man sometimes covered those of the wolf and vice-versa.

He stood, grinning, recognizing these were the tracks of the two couples that had been at the village of the Nez Percé. The group with the woman that had taken down his friend Bruno. And maybe the other woman was the young one he tangled with, he thought as he chuckled to himself. *Bruno's gonna want to know about this! He would really like another chance at that woman!*

***

Gabe used his sash to tie the wounded man to his back as they sat on the saddle aboard Ebony. He was in and out of consciousness and very weak and they could move faster with him erect and riding double with Gabe than using a travois. Ezra led the way with Dove alongside as they took to the trail just after mid-day. Cougar Woman was beside Gabe, keeping watch on the wounded man. The trail was wide and for the most part, an easy one, at least until both the creek and the trail had to cut through a series of opposing ridges that pushed into the narrow valley. But soon the hills lay back, the valley began to widen and trees receded, making the travel much easier.

Dusk was approaching when the valley opened and the hillsides showed the scars of an old fire that had turned the lush forest into a myriad of burnt stumps and downed trees. The black wounds were surrounded by new growth contrasting the light green with the remnants of the ancient conflagration. The stream, fed by several runoff creeks, had widened and offered many bends with undercut banks that harbored trout, making Ezra's mouth water for some fresh fish for supper. He looked back, "How's he doin'?" Cougar looked at the man, nodded to Ezra and lifted her hand to indicate the man was alright.

"I think we'll make camp hereabouts, maybe catch some trout for supper, whatsay?"

"Sounds good!" called out Gabe, anxious to be free of his burden. Ezra led the way to a cluster of cottonwoods and willows, liked what he saw and stepped down. The others followed his lead and Ezra helped lift the wounded man from behind Gabe. He stirred as they carried him to some blankets laid out by Dove but did not totally revive as they lay him down. While Cougar Woman tended the man, Ezra joined Gabe to strip the horses.

As the women began preparations for the evening meal, Gabe and Ezra started for the stream, Ezra with a fresh cut willow pole and his line and hook and some fresh-dug worms. Gabe preferred his familiar way of hand fishing and left Ezra at a likely looking hole and went to a bend in the creek with an undercut bank. He bellied down and slowly slipped his hand and arm into the water, feeling his way until he felt the familiar touch of fins. He slowly moved his hand along the belly of the trout until he felt the gill fins, those fins right behind the gills. He cautiously closed his fingers around the fish right behind the gills, then with a quick grip, slipped the fingers into the gills and brought the flopping fish up and tossed it on the grass.

He repeated his action several times on two more bends with undercut banks, then went back to retrieve his catch. With a willow branch that had a fork of another branch at the base, he slipped the trout, each one about fifteen to sixteen inches long and showing the circled red spots of a brook trout, onto the stick. He sat down on a gravel bar next to the water and began cleaning the fish, all twelve of them, until Ezra approached carrying four more, none as sizeable as those of Gabe.

Ezra looked at his friend and the fish, "See there. You went and got all those, now you have to clean 'em! That's why I got fewer and smaller ones, easier to clean and I won't be all night just guttin' fish!"

He sat down beside his friend and slipped his knife from the sheath at his belt and began splitting them open, chuckling as Gabe laughed at his friend. "If you liked catching 'em as much as you like eatin' 'em, you'd have twice as many!"

Ezra didn't answer, stopped moving and hissed at his friend. "Uh, ya might wanna share your catch!" as he nodded to a big shadow across the little stream.

Gabe looked up, saw a big black bear that stood watching them and sniffing the air. Dusk had dropped its curtain and the moon was just rising and Gabe knew the black bear was not known for its great eyesight. He elbowed Ezra and the men slowly stood.

There were two fish yet to be cleaned, lying on the gravel and Gabe bent to pick them up, keeping his eyes on the bear and moving very slowly. He picked up the larger fish, tossed it toward the bear and as it landed at the big bear's feet, he tossed the second. It landed beside the other and the bear dropped to his haunches and started sniffing at the fish, then took one in his mouth. Gabe and Ezra backed away, then turned and ran to camp.

They were laughing as they came into the fire-light, fish dangling at their sides. They handed off their catch to the women and Ezra explained their adventure. Dove looked past them to see if the bear had followed, but the shadows were unmoving and the men were certain the bear would devour their offering and be happy, staying on the far side of the creek. As they seated themselves near the fire, Cougar nodded toward the man on the blankets, "He roused a little bit, asked for water, then said his village is near, before the confluence. But that was all he said before he was gone again."

"Before the confluence?" asked Gabe.

"Ummhmm, and if I remember right, down there," pointing downstream of the valley, "this stream will join the Bitterroot river and it flows north to join the river some call the Salish river. That might be what he meant," explained Cougar Woman.

"So, it shouldn't be too far, then," offered Gabe.

Cougar shrugged as she rolled the fish in the cornmeal and lay them in the frying pan. The women had put some bitterroot and biscuit root in the coals earlier and the dutch oven was baking some cornmeal biscuits and of course the men were already sipping on the hot coffee. The men had started talking about their plans to go north when the wounded man stirred, moaning and mumbling. Cougar rose and went to his side, then spoke to him, prompting Gabe and Ezra to come close.

"He said he is *Ql'ispé,* Kalispel."

Gabe spoke up and in Salish said, "My name is Spirit Bear. What is your name?"

"I am Lame Bull."

"You said earlier that it was the Blackfoot that attacked your family. How many?"

"Two hands, maybe more. I had gone to get meat and when I returned, they were leaving, but one saw me, shouted and when I turned, several shot me. I fell down the ravine and later crawled away."

"They probably figured you for dead. You almost were. We will take you to your village if we can find it," suggested Gabe.

"It is on the west side of the river before it meets the bigger river from the east. Not far, half day."

Dove brought some food from the fire, handed him the plate, but he could not hold it and was weakening as he lay his head back. Cougar lifted his head and fed him a few bites of fish and biscuit root, but after a drink of water, he lay back and slept.

Gabe looked at Ezra, "Well, at least we know where the village is, we'll make it in the morning, I reckon."

"That still leaves the problem of the Frenchies," stated Ezra.

Gabe shook his head, "Yeah, don't it though."

Gabe followed Wolf back to the camp. He had been atop a long ridge that rose above the valley for his usual time with his Lord and his morning reconnoiter of the area. There was no sign of the Voyageurs and it was shaping up to be a fine day. The sky was devoid of clouds, showing its azure blue canopy as a blessing to the travelers. Cougar Woman met him with a steaming cup of coffee as he lifted his eyes to the first color of the sunrise. She handed him a platter of food and he sat to partake, with her by his side. "So, how's little Bobcat this morning?"

She smiled, "Hungry, as usual." She glanced to the side where the boy lay belly down and buck naked on a blanket.

"He sure is growing fast!" observed Gabe, looking at his son with pride. He took another bite of the strip steak, followed by the remaining bit of biscuit.

He washed it down with coffee that was hot enough to blister a lip and strong enough to last all day. He smiled at Cougar, "You did a good job!"

"With breakfast?" she asked.

"That too, but I meant with Bobcat. He's gonna be a fine man someday," he explained, looking at the boy with a smile growing. "If he learns to wear clothes, that is."

Cougar Woman tittered, "It is the way with little ones. He will be in the cradleboard soon enough."

He glanced to his left, saw the blankets where Lame Bull slept and turned to Cougar with a frown, but she answered before he asked. "He is up, he ate and went to the bushes for his morning ritual. He is weak but should ride today."

"Good. We'll adjust the packs on the Buckskin mare and let him ride her. If we're as close to his village as he thinks, he should lead us into the village, so they'll know we're friendly."

***

The trail took them due east for a little over three miles until the hills pushed in again, making the valley bottom no more than the meandering stream and the trail that rode the shoulder of the bald-faced hills on the north edge. Another three miles and the nearby hills retreated, widening the valley and revealing the broader valley before them. Lame Bull motioned to the left and led them north around the low shoulder of the mountain, over a saddle crossing of a ridge, that revealed the Bitterroot river had bent around the ridge and pointed them north. The wide lush valley lay like an emerald necklace along the base of the bald hills, where the river pushed against the slopes and crowded the trail to ride the shoulder above the water. When they dropped off the shoulder, Lame Bull reined up and motioned for everyone to step down.

Gabe looked around, saw the trees that lined the river, then the cattails waving in the breeze as they surrounded what appeared to be backwater pools left by high water from the river. The stagnant water, mostly covered with moss and patches of blooming lilies, also had several ducks lazily paddling around the edge. One leading a flock of at least ten fuzzy ducklings behind her.

Lame Bull stepped close, twisting and bending as he fought against the pain of his wounds, then pointed to a rocky and timbered finger that extended from the hills, "My village is just beyond that ridge."

As Gabe looked to the ridge, he could make out several small tendrils of smoke rising into the still morning sky. He nodded, then asked, "How many lodges in your village?"

Lame Bull frowned, and Gabe realized the language of the Kalispel was a slightly different dialect from what he had learned of the Salish. He spoke again, using sign to accompany his words and Lame Bull nodded, then answered, "Four or five double hands."

Gabe nodded, thinking *Forty or fifty lodges, that's a big village. Could be as many as two hundred or more people.* They had allowed the horses to drink at river's edge, then stepped back and let them have a few mouthfuls of grass as they talked.

Lame Bull said, "My people will accept you as friends. We have always welcomed visitors and traders to our village and invite them to stay as long as they wish." He glanced to the packs on the horses and mule, then asked, "Are you traders?"

"Sometimes. We do have some trade goods, but we're just traveling and exploring, meeting new people."

Lame Bull looked at Gabe, a slight frown wrinkling his forehead as he tried to understand this white man. He asked, "You are called Spirit Bear, but you are a white man. How did you get the name Spirit Bear?"

Gabe smiled, "Many summers ago we wintered with the Arapaho people and we helped them fight against their enemies. The chief said I was like the Spirit Bear his father knew in the north, the one that has a coat the same color as my hair and he gave me that name. He also gave Ezra his name of Black Buffalo."

"They are good names," he pointed with his chin to the grizzly claw necklace at Gabe's throat, "and I see you have taken the great bear of the mountains."

Gabe nodded, then turned toward the others, "Best mount up, we're almost there. Lame Bull says his village is just over that ridge yonder."

***

As they rounded the point, Lame Bull reined up and explained, "This is the summer camp of my people. In the winter, our camp is further north and in the mountains. Our winter lodges are mostly earth lodges or covered with tule and earth. This is a good place," he summarized as he gigged his mount forward.

Gabe and the others saw the village tucked into a cove of flat land meadow, surrounded on three sides by mature timber. Behind the village the timber covered hills rose to meet the distant Bitterroot mountains. On the east, a peninsula of land extended just over a mile to meet the big bend of the river. Just less than a mile wide, it was framed by trees that rode the bank of the river as it bent around the point and held a wide meadow of tall grass where the herd of horses grazed. A few lifted their heads to see the newcomers, but soon lost interest and continued their graze, watched over by several young men who also watched the riders with curiosity.

Gabe and Cougar Woman rode behind Lame Bull as they entered the edge of the camp, but word had

already spread of visitors coming and many stood
beside their hide tipis, watching the group as they
rode into the village. Wolf trotted between Gabe and
Cougar Woman and the youngsters excitedly pointed
him out and jabbered with their friends and mothers
as they looked at the big black beast, a rare sight for
most. As they approached the center of the village, the
customary central compound was open and usually
held a few cookfires, but there were many people busy
at trader's blankets. About a half-dozen white men,
traders, tended the blankets, making trades with the
villagers and few were concerned with more visitors.

Gabe saw a familiar face, nodded his direction, and
leaned back to speak to Ezra, "See somebody familiar?" he asked, grinning.

Ezra frowned, looked at the different traders, then
a slow smile began, "Ain't that David Thompson?"

"Ummhmm, sure is!" answered Gabe, but before
he could say more, Lame Bull stopped and slid down
from his mount to stand before the man that was obviously the leader of the village. The two men talked
animatedly at length, then paused and the chief looked
up at Gabe, motioned him to step down and watched
as the tall man in buckskins stepped to the ground.
Lame Bull turned toward him and said, "This is Bear
Track, the leader of our village. He," pointing to a
man that sided the chief, "is Big Canoe, our Shaman."

The men nodded to Gabe and as Lame Bull introduced him, motioned the others to get down, and introduced each one. Bear Track glanced from Gabe to Cougar Woman and said to both, "Lame Bull has told how you helped him and brought him back to our village. We are grateful to you and ask that you stay with us and join in our activities."

Gabe nodded, then with a bit of a frown he looked to Lame Bull, "Did you tell about the Blackfoot?"

"Yes, he knows."

Gabe looked from Lame Bull to the chief and said, "We are grateful to you as well. We would like to stay with your people for a short while." He nodded toward the traders, "We know the man you trade with and will visit with him as well."

"It is good," answered the chief, then turning to Lame Bull, "You will show them to the lodge of your family?"

Lame Bull dropped his eyes, then nodded, "Yes."

He turned toward Gabe, reached for the reins of the buckskin and motioned for them to follow. The lodge was near the north edge of the village, close to the trees that lined the river and was a large hide lodge. The peak was darkened with many cookfires within and the flaps were opened to the north. The buckskin covered opening faced the east and Lame Bull flipped it aside and stepped in, pausing as he stood. He turned back and spoke to Gabe, "I will need to remove some things of my family before you enter.

If you like, you may take your horses to the herd and let them graze with the others."

Gabe nodded, motioned to Ezra and the men stripped the horses, stacking their gear beside the lodge while Lame Bull tended to the personal items of his family. Once the gear was stacked, the men took the horses to the meadow and Ezra asked, "So, how long you expect to stay?"

"Dunno. I'd like to visit with Thompson, see what their plans are and let him know about the Hudson's Bay bunch. Sooner or later we're gonna have to face the Voyageurs. I ain't interested in trying to keep runnin' from 'em. They might not be interested in us at all, then again . . ."

"Yeah, then again says a lot," replied Ezra.

"I remember you! You're the one that traded us outta that sturgeon nose canoe, said you were goin' down the Missouri to St. Louis, wasn't it?"

"That's right," answered a grinning Gabe as he stretched out his hand to shake with David Thompson.

"Let me see, it was Stone, Gabe Stone, isn't it?" he asked, standing to shake hands.

"That's right. You've a good memory. We only met on those couple days in the early fall, let me think, little over two years ago!" said Gabe, remembering a less than pleasant time in his life.

"And you had just lost your wife, if I remember correctly. But didn't I see you and your company ride in and you had another woman and a baby, didn't you?"

"You're very observant. Yes, she is my wife and the mother of my first son. Cougar Woman is her name, Shoshone."

"So, what're you doin' way up north in this country?" asked Thompson, sitting down to continue his trading and offering Gabe and Ezra a seat beside him.

"Bout the same thing as you, just exploring and discovering new country and new people. We ran onto a fella back up the trail from this village, brought him back and gonna stay a while. How 'bout you?"

"Much the same. Exploring the country, trying to map as much of it as I can, making new contacts with new people." He nodded to the other traders, "We're all with the Northwest company and been out a couple months now. It's been good. Dealt with the Gros Ventre, Blackfoot, Kutenai, Coeur D'Alene, couple other bands of the Kalispel. We might make a swing through the Nez Percé. We're about loaded down now, we'll hafta trade for some more packhorses if we go much further and I like them spotted ponies of the Nez Percé," explained Thompson.

Gabe looked around at the other traders and their wares as they dealt with the natives, then looked back at Thompson. "How're you getting along with the Hudson's Bay people?"

Thompson cocked his head to the side, a slight frown crossing his face, "I suspect you've a special reason for asking that, am I right?"

"Perhaps, so, how are you getting along?"

"Not too well. After I spent so many years with 'em, then left for Northwest, we haven't been too friendly. Both sides have claimed the others have jumped 'em and stolen pelts, but best I can make out, it's just a renegade bunch of the Bay people that's causing the problems. So, what're you thinking?" asked Thompson.

"We had a run in with 'em when we were with the Nez Percé. One of their number had attacked and killed a woman, then tried to attack my woman and her friend. Although he was a mountain of a man, Cougar Woman took him down, cut him up, but let him go. Last we saw, the Nez Percé had him and the rest of the Bay people had hightailed it. But . . . we thought they went back towards the Columbia, until we saw them coming along behind us."

"They're headin' this way?" asked Thompson.

"Ummhmm, 'bout a day behind us."

"How many?"

"Bout eight or ten, depending on what the warriors under Twisted Hair did to the bunch. But from what I could tell, there's still at least eight, maybe more. I didn't feel like hanging around to count 'em."

"They have somethin' against you?" asked Thompson.

"I let the chief know about the one that was killed and the big 'un that did it."

"What was the leader's name, y'know?"

"Adrien Laurent, black beard and eyes, broad shoulders, buckskins and a fur hat with a big feather in it. He wasn't happy about me doin' what I did. He thought as a white man I should figger the natives as expendable," explained Gabe, drawing his knees up and wrapping his arms around them, clasping his hands together. He had felt a chill run down his back and glanced around, looking for any warning of danger, but the village was peaceful.

"That sounds like the same bunch. Not sure about the name, but names are changed more often than their underwear up here!"

Ezra leaned forward, "How many men you have?"

He nodded toward the other traders, "The six of us, two more back with the horses and gear. But we're all tired out, been out a couple months, moving all the time, haven't had a good day's rest since I don't know when." He looked around, then back at Gabe and Ezra, "Does chief Bear Track know about the Bay people comin' this way?"

"Not yet. I wanted to see what your plans were first. How long are you staying around?" asked Gabe.

"We were planning on leaving first thing in the morning, taking the river trail to the Nez Percé, but . . ." he paused, shaking his head. "I'll have to talk to the rest of the men, let 'em know what we're up against. They've been talking about making this our last stop before turning back and headin' home."

***

Henri Petit was sitting on the bank of the creek beside Bruno. The big man looked at his little friend, "You are sure it's the same woman?"

"Don't you remember, they had a big wolf with them?"

"Yeah, why?"

"That's how I know it was them. There were wolf tracks all around that camp, both on top of the man's tracks and stepped on by the man. They were together alright and I've not seen any other pet wolves with a traveling family, have you?"

"No!" spat Bruno. He kicked at a stone at the creek's edge, knocking it into the water. He looked down at Henri, letting a slow grin paint his face, "I'm gonna enjoy that woman, more'n any other. After I'm done, then I'll rip her apart and feed her to her wolf!" hehehe, he giggled, making his rotund middle bounce as he laughed.

He sobered, then growled, "Does Adrien know they're the same bunch?"

"Yeah, an' he kinda grinned about it. According to Bernard, he wasn't too happy when that lanky fella told the chief about the dead girl, told him he shouldn'ta done it, coz he was a white man and she was just an Indian."

"So, he might be willing to let me have my way with his woman, huh?"

The sly little man cackled, thinking about the

vicious manner of his friend and answered, "Yeah, I think so! He don't like nobody messin' with his men, even you!"

Slobber drooled down the whiskers of the big man as he thought about the woman that had cut him and all he could think about was his personal vengeance. She cut him, he wanted to cut her! He shook his head and laughed at his own thoughts and the images he conjured up in his imagination.

***

"I think there's another one with 'em. The sign at that last camp showed one of 'em was injured, bled a lot, but there's still the same number of horses. They're more'n a day ahead of us," explained the little man, still guiding for the group.

"Still think they're headed for the Bitterroot?" asked Adrien.

"If that's where this creek leads, then yeah."

"You keep a close eye, make sure nobody leaves the bunch and if you find out anything more, you hurry on back and let me know," ordered the leader of the Voyageurs.

The sun was to their back, lowering over the mountains, when they rode from the valley. Before them was the Bitterroot river, winding its way down the wide verdant valley. Adrien signaled the men to follow as he turned his mount north to follow the trail that sided the river. They had gone less than a mile when Henri Petit sat in the middle of the trail, waiting. As the two leaders, Adrien and Gaston rode up to him, he nodded, "There's a village of Kalispel just beyond that rocky ridge behind me. It's a good-sized village, most of forty lodges."

"Did they see you?" asked Gaston.

"Don't think so, I didn't see any dog soldier types patrolling around, but you know them Injuns, they coulda seen us comin' miles ago!"

"You're grinning. What else?" asked Adrien.

"Looks like some Northwest boys tradin' with 'em," said Henri, a sadistic grin splitting his face.

"Any sign of that bunch with the women?" asked Gaston.

"Their trail leads to the camp, but I dunno if they're still there. Didn't wanna go around the village to see if there were any tracks leavin'."

Gaston looked over their left shoulder, "That sun's 'bout gone. We either pitch camp hereabouts or ride on into the village."

Adrien looked at his second, slowly nodding and thinking, "Might be best to wait till morning. Maybe mouse there can get another look, tell us more, before we enter the village." He glanced at their scout, then to his second and added, "If Northwest has been trading with 'em, it might be easier to just pass the village and hit the traders on the trail. That way, we get the rest of their goods, all the pelts and not hafta trade our goods off, leaving more for the next village."

Gaston did not like it. It had never been his way to waylay other traders, having been an independent trapper and trader, he knew how hard it was to accumulate enough of anything just to get by, much less get rich. But he had to yield to what Adrien ordered, otherwise he would forfeit his share of their take on this entire trip and this was his last chance to get enough to make his way and leave the mountains. He had long dreamed of having a trading post or general store in warmer climes with a good woman beside him and at his age, he could not be choosy as to how he would get his stake to make his way. Gaston reined around, motioned for the men to make camp in the cottonwoods beside the river and led the way himself.

19 / SHOCK

Jean-Phillipe Fabron, the libertine of the bunch, was standing guard, but believed there was no danger and decided to sit a spell and enjoy his meerschaum pipe with the last of his tobacco. He chose the big ponderosa at the edge of the trees and seated himself, leaning back against the rough bark and slipping his pipe from his pocket, his tobacco pouch from the other. The camp was well obscured in the trees and with no fire for the night and the horses on a picket line, he assumed all was safe. He lay the bit of char cloth between his legs and covered it with a little tinder, then struck steel to the flint and brought sparks. It only took two tries and the char cloth glowed with the tiny rim of fire, he held his hands on the sides of the little bit, blowing gently to bring the flame and the tinder caught. He had laid his cape over his legs to shield the flame and with his pipe packed, he brought a small stick with a flame to the bowl. With two deep draws, the tobacco caught and he drew deeply of the smoke, savored it a moment and slowly let it slip from his lips.

The moon was waning from full and Jean-Phillipe looked high overhead to see it tuck itself behind the thick cloud cover. As it hid itself, the shadow of darkness fell upon the valley before him, giving him added comfort with the blanket of black. He leaned back his head, felt a piece of the shaggy bark fall into his collar and he leaned forward to dig out the rough bit. But as he moved, he caught movement at the river. He had watched the light of the moon bounce off the ripples of the water, but now that it was in the clouds, there were no reflections, but there was movement. He unconsciously leaned forward, squinting his eyes, and saw riders silhouetted against the pale sandbar, many riders.

The Voyageurs had made their camp well back in the trees at the edge of a cut between the buttes and Jean-Phillipe knew he could not be seen, unless he moved. He watched, noting the images and trying to determine what tribe. They certainly were not the Kalispel, he thought. He looked to the dim glow of the moon, guessing it to be less than two hours before first light. With a few having the tall standing headdress and others with feathers at the back, but standing forward, he was certain these were Blackfoot and at this time of night, up to no good.

He slowly rolled to the side and using the trees as cover, he went to the sleeping blankets of Adrien and Gaston. He nudged them awake and motioned for silence. He nodded toward the river and whispered, "Looks like a big band of Blackfoot, getting ready to hit the village yonder."

Both men sat up, reaching for their rifles and pouches. Adrien asked, "Did they see you?"

"No, I don't think so. It's darker'n the inside of a deep cave out there."

Adrien looked at Gaston, "What do you think?"

"Not our affair," answered Gaston. "But . . ."

"But what?" retorted Adrien, tossing aside his blankets and standing. He glowered at Gaston as he too stood.

"If they hit 'em hard, that'll also do in the Northwest boys and all the peltries you were thinkin' of takin'."

"Are you thinkin' we should help? Maybe sound the alarm?" asked Adrien.

Gaston shrugged, "That's up to you."

***

The low growl brought Gabe instantly awake. He peered through slit eyes to examine the interior of the lodge where the others were sleeping. He had developed the practice of not moving when he first came awake but making certain of his surroundings with a quick look around. Wolf had padded to the entry flap, looking over his shoulder for Gabe who quickly slipped from the blankets, rifle in hand and stuffing his pistol in his belt. He slung the horn and possibles pouch over his shoulder as he pushed through the blanket, stepping to the side to view the village. All appeared quiet, as he glanced down to Wolf who stared toward the lower part of the village and the river beyond.

Ezra pushed through the entry, rifle in hand and looked at Gabe then Wolf. "What's happenin'?" he whispered.

"Dunno. Wolf's detected somethin'." He glanced over his shoulder at the slight rise behind the village, "I'm goin' high for a look-see!" he whispered and with a wave of his hand, started Wolf ahead of him as he trotted to the trees. Ezra stayed by the lodge, dropping to one knee at the side of the entry, making a lower shadow in the darkness.

Directly behind the lodges at the edge of the village, the tall trees offered shade and windbreak for the nearby lodges, but Gabe wanted to see more and trotted through the trees, moving as silent as a mountain lion as he followed Wolf. The two quickly made a promontory and turned to look over the village. The moon began to peek out from the dark clouds and the line of dim light showed at the edge of the camp. Beyond the camp and in the meadow below, the horse herd grazed, but even at this distance, Gabe could see several horses standing, heads up and looking toward the end of the rocky ridge and the river beyond.

Gabe knew if an attack was to come, that would be the logical point of attack. The meadow at the east end with the horse herd would cause the horses to alarm the village with their whinnying and more, on the north edge, a long rock butte made a surprise attack impossible, but there on the south edge where he looked, that would be the point. And he saw movement! Many horses and riders, coming from the water where a long sandbar shone white in the dim light.

He had little time and instantly rose and started at a run back through the trees. As he approached the lodge with the women, he shouted, "Blackfoot! Attack!" He was not certain they were Blackfoot, but it seemed the only possibility. Ezra jumped up, but Gabe hollered, "Stay with the women! I'm headin' to warn the others!" He quickly dug at the stack of gear for his saddle and the pistols in the saddle holsters. He stuffed them in his belt and took off at a run.

As he ran through the village, he shouted in Salish, "Blackfoot! Blackfoot!"

People quickly roused, warriors coming from the lodges armed and looking, but within moments, gunfire from the lower end of the village told of the attack. Warriors ran toward the attack, nocking arrows as they ran. The Blackfoot were known to have trade fusils, similar to the smoothbore rifle used in the Revolutionary War, obtained from the Hudson Bay company in trade for pelts. But there were a few of the Kalispel that were also armed with the rifle and the rattle of musketry was heard. The moon showed its face just in time for the defenders to pick their targets and the surprise had been tampered by Gabe's warning.

He followed the main trail that led from the river to the central compound of the village. With the compound at his back, he had his first sight of the attackers, Gabe stopped and lifted his rifle, sighted on the nearest Blackfoot and pulled the trigger. The Ferguson bucked and spat lead, but Gabe dropped the rifle down and spun the trigger guard to start his reload. He was well-experienced with this weapon and he let loose a steady barrage, sending one lead messenger of death after another, an average of about ten seconds apart. He was blocking the primary access to the rest of the village, believing the main force of the attack would come directly at him and he stood his ground.

Then Ezra was at his side, and Gabe glanced with a frown at the man, "I thought you were staying with the women!"

Without wasting a motion or a second of time, the

men spoke as they fired and reloaded, "Who do you think sent me down here! You don't really think anybody's gonna get in that lodge with them two, do you?" In spite of the blow back powder blacking his face, Gabe grinned, "No, reckon not!"

But the greater number of armed warriors of the Blackfoot was pushing into the village and before Gabe could lift his rifle, a screaming Blackfoot charged, tomahawk raised overhead. Gabe lifted the butt of his rifle to smash it against the ear of the warrior, knocking him senseless and smashing his cheek against his teeth, knocking several out and splattering blood from his mouth and ear as he crashed to the ground.

Ezra hollered, "Look out!" as a mounted warrior with a lance raised and ready to throw thundered toward them. Gabe rolled to the side, grabbing at a pistol as he did, cocking the weapon as he came to his knees and fired at the screaming warrior. The bullet took him in the throat, blowing out the back of his neck and driving him off the horse. But more were coming right behind and Gabe spun the double barrels and cocked the second hammer, firing at the low-lying warrior that straddled a bright colored paint horse, the mane flying in his face. The bullet burrowed its way into the top of the man's head, splattering blood on the mane of the horse as the man's death grip twisted in the long hair.

Ezra fired his Lancaster rifle, unseated a Black-foot, then dropped the rifle at his feet as he pulled his pistol. With no wasted motion, he brought it to bear on a warrior that straddled a Kalispel woman, ready to split her skull with a tomahawk, and fired. The bullet took the man just below his exposed armpit and traveled through his body to exit his rib cage, having exploded the man's heart as it drove through. The man rolled to the side, dead before he hit the ground and the woman scampered to her feet, running for her lodge.

Gabe stood with the two saddle pistols in his hands, picking his targets, first to fire was the right hand big pistol that spat fire and smoke as it sent the lead ball to penetrate the chest of a Blackfoot, readying his shot with his bow. But the impact of the bullet sent the arrow wobbling away as the warrior sat down, dead. The men stood side by side, Ezra reloading his double barrel as Gabe fired and Gabe reloading as Ezra fired.

Both men thought the Blackfoot were gaining until a barrage of rifle fire from the edge of the rocky ridge on the south edge of the camp racketed through the valley. Gabe glanced that way, but the dim light of early morning revealed little, but it was unmistakable rifle fire and plenty of it. Ezra had looked the same way and asked, "Now, who do you suppose that is?"

"Dunno, but they are turning the tide, I do believe," answered Gabe, taking another shot. The bodies were piling up around them and they continually moved among the lodges, needing to get away from the low-lying powder smoke just to see what they were shooting at, picking each position as the attackers charged. The shrieking of warriors and wailing of women added to the cacophony of the battle. Gunshots, dogs barking, horses screeching and the thunder of hooves filled the valley with the noise of the fight. Wolf repeatedly came to his feet, wanting to lunge into the fray, but stayed at Gabe's side, restrained by his friend.

20 / BATTLE

Gabe dropped his eyes to his reloading for just an instant and Wolf lunged before him, taking down a Blackfoot, teeth at his throat, as his one hundred fifty plus pounds drove at his chest and rode him to the ground. With a snarl and a twist of his head, the big black wolf ripped the throat from the attacker and stood astraddle of the body, looking for another one. There was fighting and screaming all over the village. Many of the Blackfoot had gone to ground and were scattering through the village, attacking at will and ransacking lodges, killing anyone that resisted.

Gabe glanced to his side to see Ezra in the grips of a fight with tomahawks. The brawny Blackfoot was the equal of Ezra in size, but the strength of Black Buffalo was unmatched. Each man held a hawk in one hand and gripped the wrist of his enemy with the other. They struggled against each other, the Blackfoot a little taller as he tried to rise up on his toes to drive his weight against Ezra, but it was not to happen as Ezra drew air, widened his stance and pushed up against the man. The Blackfoot had probably never met his match and the surprise and fear showed in his eyes as Ezra lunged forward, lifting the man off his feet and driving him to his back as he thrust his knee to the warrior's crotch, burying the blade of his hawk between the man's eyes. Ezra wrenched his hawk free and drove it down again to split the man's skull.

As Ezra jerked his hawk free, he looked for another foe, turned toward a warrior that was coming from his right, but recognized him as Lame Bull and lowered his hawk to his side. The Blackfoot appeared to be withdrawing and Lame Bull stood beside the men, looking at the carnage before them. An arrow whispered past Ezra's ear and he spun to see the shooter nocking another arrow. Ezra pushed Bull aside and snatched his pistol up, cocking and firing in one quick movement. The bullet flew true and shattered the sternum of the Blackfoot, driving the man to his back and loosing the arrow into the air.

Gabe finished reloading his pistols as he watched the tide of battle turn. The few Blackfoot that were still mounted, lifted others behind them as they turned away, slapping heels to the ribs of the horses to lunge and take to a gallop. They lay low on the necks of the horses, using bows and lances to slap the rumps of the mounts to run. Arrows arched overhead toward the runaways, one impaled itself in the rear of a retreating horse, causing it to kick and buck, unseating his rider.

Gabe stuffed the pistols in his belt and bent for his rifle, when a screaming Blackfoot came from behind him, throwing himself on Gabe's back and driving him to the ground. The warrior straddled Gabe's back, pushing with his free hand and raising his tomahawk with the other, ready to strike but Wolf lunged and caught the man's arm in his teeth and with a snarl he tore a hunk of flesh from the man's arm as he screamed his surprise and pain. Then Gabe bucked and rolled, knocking the man to the ground on his back, but Wolf would not be deterred and went for the man's throat, ripping and tearing, as he growled and snarled. The man's screams were stifled and he went limp in death, blood covering his face and chest and the ground beside him.

Gabe came to his feet, pistol in hand, looking for any other attackers. He drew a deep breath, looked at Ezra and Lame Bull and said, "Is it over?"

"Mebbe," responded Ezra, glancing from Gabe to Lame Bull. The Kalispel warrior nodded his head and looked at the two men, "You have killed many Blackfoot," nodding toward the bodies that lay before them. Gabe and Ezra did not respond and Lame Bull said, "You have helped my people, we are grateful." He looked at his friends again, then added, "I must see to my friends." Gabe and Ezra nodded, and Lame Bull walked away.

They were vigilant as they saw several of the Kalispel warriors working their way among the downed and dead of the Blackfoot. Showing no mercy, any that were wounded were quickly dispatched and any weapons or other useful items taken. Many of the Blackfoot had rifles gained in trade with the Hudson Bay traders and the weapons were prized and seized by the Kalispel. Gabe glanced at Ezra, "They're takin' those rifles, but there's probably not a one among them that knows how to load a rifle, much less shoot it!"

"Yeah, but it's a prize of battle for them and they'll probably figure it out, maybe get some passerby white man to show them how," he declared, looking sidelong at his friend with a grin.

The men turned away and started back to the far edge of the village to the lodge that was their temporary home, leaving the pillaging of the dead to the Kalispel. They held their rifles across their chests, looking about as they walked. There had been a few lodges set afire when they were dropped on the cookfires within and now were just blackened piles of smoldering hides and frames. They passed one lodge where a woman sat with her man's head in her lap, bloody chest showing tomahawk wounds, as she wailed over his death. As they neared their lodge, they saw Cougar Woman sitting inside, the entry flap thrown up so she could see the path into the village and when she spotted the men returning, she came from the tipi, smiling and with Bobcat in her arms as he nursed.

Gabe wrapped his free arm around her and pulled her close as Ezra ducked into the hide lodge, greeted by Dove as he disappeared. "Was it Blackfoot?" asked Cougar, looking at Gabe.

"Yeah. Probably the same bunch and more that jumped Lame Bull and his family. The first bunch was probably scouting out the country, saw Bull and his family leaving and followed them to the hot springs."

"There was a lot of rifle fire, I didn't think the Kalispel had many rifles," stated Cougar.

"Yeah, I'm not sure what that was. It came from the ridge to the south and helped send the Blackfoot runnin'. Reckon we'll find out soon enough."

The sun was peeking above the eastern hills and bending its golden lances over the higher peaks. The line of sunlight lit the lodges at the back edge of the village first, then drew the light down toward the river. Gabe stood before the lodge, facing the new day and looking into the village, hearing the rising sounds of women wailing the loss of their men. He held Cougar Woman tight beside him, looked down at her, "I think I'll go to the mountain."

She nodded, releasing him, knowing he was going

to spend some time with his Lord. She looked up at her man with loving eyes, "May I come with you?"

He smiled, "Of course," then looked down at the little one in her arms, "Bobcat asleep?"

"No, but I'll use my blanket carry and he soon will be."

When she stepped from the lodge, the blanket was over one shoulder and the babe was cradled before her. She handed Gabe a wet cloth, smiling, "You are as dark as Ezra, the powder."

Gabe grinned and wiped his face, looking at the black powder smoke residue that had been a blow-back from the battle. He wiped again and more thoroughly, then smiled at Cougar who nodded her approval. They walked slowly and quietly through the trees, taking a familiar trail to the crest of the hill directly behind and to the west of the village. It was always tiring to be in any battle like the one this morning and the weight of taking the lives of so many was heavy upon him and he needed the time with the Lord to recoup.

Before, he had stopped on the crest of the shoulder to the south of the mount, but now pushed on toward the summit. The hilltop showed timber on the north side but held only scattered piñon and cedar on the south face. At the crest were several flat boulders, Wolf had led the way and stopped by a large boulder and dropped to his belly to wait for them. They seated themselves on the rock, hanging their feet off the side and leaned back together.

Gabe slipped his Bible from his sash and leaning on one elbow, opened the book, flipped the pages to where he wanted, then turned it to Cougar Woman. "Here ya go, practice your reading!" he said as he pointed to the selected passage.

She began, "*But they that wait upon the Lord shall renew their strength; they shall mount up with wings as eagles; they shall run, and not be weary; and they shall walk and not faint.*"

She looked at Gabe, back at the scripture, and said, "I like that!" and paused, then asked, "To wait, is that just like sitting and waiting?"

Gabe smiled, "No, that is getting out of God's way and letting Him show himself in our lives, to control what happens and what we do. It's like when you're riding and you scoot back so He can get in front and take the reins to go where He wants instead of you."

"So, when He's in control, all the rest applies to us, the wings as eagles and more?"

Gabe nodded, "and more." He took her hand in his and began to pray, thanking God for keeping them safe during the fight and so much more. When he finished with an 'Amen,' he squeezed her hand and sat up, looking at the village below. As he watched, he frowned when he saw several riders come around the south bluff and start toward the camp. He could tell these were not attacking Blackfoot, but he was thinking they were the Voyageurs with Hudson Bay. He pointed them out to Cougar, "I think those are the ones that were shooting from the bluff and I'm thinkin' they are the traders with Hudson Bay."

"Are they following us? But I thought you said the big one was in the hands of the Nez Percé?"

"They were behind us on the trail here, but if they're following us, I don't know. And the big one was bound to the rack in the village of the Nez Percé when I last saw him, so he's probably not with them," said Gabe. But he also knew it was possible the man had broken free and returned to his friends. If so, Gabe knew he might be forced to confront the man and at the very least to keep him away from their lodge and Cougar Woman. He spoke to Wolf, "Lead the way boy, we're goin' back," and watched as Wolf trotted off, stopping once to look back to see if they were following, then trotted on down the slope. It was steep enough so Gabe and Cougar Woman had to zigzag down and were soon in the trees, following the same trail on the return.

Dove was busy at the cookfire in front of the lodge, Ezra sat nearby with Chipmunk between his legs, pulling on the fringe of his daddy's buckskins. They looked up as Gabe and Cougar came near and Gabe was quick to say, "Looks like that rifle fire came from the Hudson Bay bunch. They're riding into the village now."

Ezra looked up at Gabe, expecting more, but he sat down and reached for a cup and the coffee pot to pour himself some of the black brew. He leaned back, pensive and Ezra asked, "Could you tell if the big'un was with 'em?"

"Nope. But I intend to find out soon enough. Maybe we'll just stroll down there to see what might be happening, ya reckon?"

21 / TRADERS

The Northwest company had been formed about twenty years prior by the Frobisher brothers, Alexander Henry, Isaac Todd, and others. Formed for the sole purpose of breaking the stranglehold of the Hudson's Bay Company on the North American Fur trade, it was headquartered in Montreal, but had bands of traders moving throughout Canada and the French and Spanish territories in America. Whenever the different companies met, there was usually some kind of conflict and often considerable bloodletting.

The Northwest company band that was in the village of the Kalispel was led by David Thompson, who had previously partnered with Alexander Henry the younger, but now had as his second, a Metis named Jacques LaRamee. Although this group had never run up against the Hudson's Bay traders before, they knew of others that had to fight their way through the lands of the different tribes of natives, always seeking to be first to trade with the many bands of the different tribes.

Gabe and Ezra stood beside Thompson and LaRamee as they watched the Voyageurs confer with the chief, Bear Track. "I don't think they'll get much; we've pretty well cleaned 'em out!" declared Thompson.

"But if you notice, they've got a crate of trade fusils and after that battle this morning, I think the men will trade just about anything to get their hands on one of them," declared Ezra.

"That's something our company is a little hesitant to get involved in, trading rifles to the natives. It could get a little hazardous if they decide to turn against us!" responded Thompson.

"I see you were getting ready to pull out, still leavin'?" asked Gabe, glancing to the lined-up pack-horses where the men were strapping packs down.

"After what you said about them at the Nez Percé, and the problems they caused, plus what we know about them hitting our traders, I think it will be to our advantage. They'll be busy here at least a day, maybe two, which will give us a good lead on 'em and make it a little safer for us," explained Thompson. As the men spoke, Gabe saw the two leaders of the Voyageurs approaching, Wolf was beside Gabe and rose, his hackles raised and a low growl rumbling. Gabe reached down to quiet him, "Easy boy, lay down now," and Wolf bellied down, but his head was lifted and he watched the Frenchmen as they came near and extended their hands to shake and introduce themselves.

"Gentlemen! I am Adrien Laurent, and this is Gaston Durand. We are with the Hudson's Bay Company."

With his hand extended, Thompson said, "I am David Thompson, and this is Jacques LaRamee. We are with the Northwest company."

The four men shook hands as Laurent looked at Gabe, frowning, "And I believe we met back at the Nez Percé camp, did we not?" He extended his hand to Gabe who accepted and shook his hand as he said, "That's right. I am Gabe Stone and this," nodding to Ezra, "is Ezra Blackwell, and we are not with any company!"

"Ahh, I see. I did not know you were traders, monsieur."

"Like I said, we're not with any company. Any trading we do is just between friends."

"And you are friends with the Kalispel?"

"Among others. We make friends wherever we go because we treat 'em right," interjected Ezra, stepping forward slightly.

The Frenchmen scowled at the comment but chose to not respond. Laurent looked back at Thompson, "I see you are leaving?"

"That's right. We've had some good trading with

these fine folks and now it's on to more."

"Are you going to the Nez Percé," inquired Laurent, smiling.

"Not rightly sure. We were considering the Blackfoot until they visited us first. But there are plenty of others," replied Thompson.

"Oui, oui, that is true. We will try to make a few trades here, then go north. You must have come from the north, is that so?"

Although it was the way with travelers in the mountains to always share news of routes, dangers, native uprisings and more, Thompson just smiled, refusing to answer the probing question, forcing the Frenchmen to turn to one another. "Well, Gaston, we must finish setting up for the trades. We have many rifles to trade to these brave warriors, so let us go." He gave a sardonic grin to the group of four, turned his back on them and returned to the circle. He knew the Northwest did not trade in rifles and he smirked, knowing the Kalispel would gladly trade anything they had left for one of the weapons.

Gabe had looked over the group that was working at the blankets and trade goods as the traders talked, noticing the absence of the big man and the mousy one. There were three men busy at the blankets, a tall rail of a man with a white streak in his hair, an overly friendly curly haired one with a red stocking cap and a younger man that was obviously the errand boy. But Gabe was certain the Voyageurs had done as before, leaving the rest of the group with the other pack horses and pelts in the camp and the other two could still be with the bunch. Once again the hackles on his neck twitched and he knew there was trouble just waiting, but he did not know from what source.

As the Frenchmen walked away, Gabe turned to Thompson, "You think they'll try to follow you?"

"Well, I'm not certain, but I think this is the same bunch I've heard about before. But the group I heard about had a big man that was a monster in a fight and his partner was a squeaky sadistic freak."

Gabe slowly lifted his head, glancing to Ezra, "This is the same bunch then. The two you mention were with 'em back at the Nez Percé camp and they're probably with the others in the camp of this bunch. He," nodding toward the retreating Laurent, "always leaves some behind with the goods they already traded for and to keep an eye on the packhorses."

Thompson glanced to LaRamee, back at Gabe, lowered his voice and turned away. "We're going south from here, along the Bitterroot River. We'll hit some of the Salish villages, maybe some Shoshone near the headwaters of the Missouri where we saw you last, then east to the Crow and north to the Assiniboine, then back to the post. When we leave here, we'll head north, then cut back south to try to throw them off our trail, but just in case, I would appreciate it if you trailed them a ways and see what they do. If they strike our trail and turn south, you'll know where to find us."

Gabe dropped his head, glanced to Ezra then back to Thompson, "You're asking a lot. We've got three little ones and our wives with us."

"I don't want you to get them in any danger, but if you would just watch . . ."

Again Gabe looked at Ezra, saw a slight nod and answered Thompson, sighed and answered, "We'll do what we can."

Thompson and LaRamee were both relieved and with a glance to their men, began to say their good-byes to Gabe and Ezra. "Here's hoping we won't see you again anytime soon!" declared Thompson.

"I'm all for that!" answered Gabe, letting a grin split his face.

With handshakes all around, the men turned away from one another and set about their tasks for the day. It was a little after mid-day and Gabe wanted to stop by the lodge of the chief to see how the village fared in the attack and what they might be planning. As they approached, the chief and the Shaman were sitting by the cookfire with Lame Bull opposite them. When they saw Gabe and Ezra they motioned for them to join the group, offering them a platter of stew prepared by Bear Track's woman.

Gabe and Ezra accepted, sat near Lame Bull and

Bear Track spoke, "Lame Bull has told us of your many kills against the Blackfoot. We are grateful for your warning and for the help in the fight."

Gabe nodded, "It was the right thing to do, we are guests in your village." He scooped a bite into his mouth, glancing at Ezra who was wasting no time consuming the offering.

"The Blackfoot know not to attack this village again. Because we were warned, our losses were few, but we killed many of the enemy and gained many horses and rifles as well."

Lame Bull added, "Because of you," nodding to both Gabe and Ezra, "and the shooters on the ridge, the battle was our win."

"About those shooters, you mean the traders with the Hudson's Bay?" asked Gabe.

"That is right," responded Bear Track.

Gabe paused a moment, then added, "We were with the Nez Percé when those men were there. One of the men killed a woman of the camp and attacked two others, one was my wife."

Bear Track and Big Canoe scowled, "But I saw your woman, she showed no marks of an attack," declared Big Canoe, the shaman.

"That's because my woman is a warrior and took the big man down, cut him up a mite, and spared him for the Nez Percé. But I think he escaped from their village and is back at the camp of the Frenchmen. I tell you this so you will be aware and watchful."

The chief glanced to his shaman and to Lame Bull, then looking at Gabe said, "We are grateful. You warned us before and we will heed this warning also."

Lame Bull questioned, "You will be leaving soon?"

"Yes. Although we are grateful for the time with your people, we want to explore more of the country and meet other people. We will probably leave come first light."

They finished the meal, tossed some scraps to Wolf, then expressed their appreciation, and rose to leave. From the central compound, the borrowed lodge was about three hundred yards and near the tree line. They followed a winding path that led to the far lodges. Wolf lunged ahead, running to the lodge. Gabe said, "Something's wrong," as he ran after Wolf, Ezra following close behind.

As they neared the lodge, they heard Chipmunk crying and sobs from Dove. Gabe threw back the skin at the entry, ducked in and saw Dove holding Squirrel, Bobcat laying on a blanket beside her. She looked up with tear-filled eyes and said, "He took her!" pointing to the entry.

"Who?"

"The big man that attacked her before! He grabbed Bobcat away from her and threw him here, on the blanket, grabbed her and jerked her to her feet, then dragged her away! He held both wrists and she couldn't fight back. She told me to stay with the babies!" Dove was sobbing as she spoke, cradling her infant at her breast.

Gabe looked at his son, back at Dove, "How long ago?"

"Just now! They can't be far!" she pointed to the trail that led to the trees. Gabe looked at her again, down at Wolf, "Find Cougar!" he shouted, pointing to the trail. It was a black streak that took to the trail toward the trees, followed by a long-legged buckskin clad ball of anger and fury!

Dove looked at Ezra, "Go!" pointing after Gabe.

22 / CHASE

"C'mon Squaw!" growled Bruno. He had Cougar Woman by her wrists, he had tried holding both with one massive paw, but she fought and kicked forcing him to hold each wrist with his bone-breaking grip. He squeezed and snarled, walking backwards, dragging her, then jerked her to her feet, swept one arm around her neck, pulling her tight against him holding her left arm in his left paw. "Now you're comin' along with me or I'll break your neck right where we stand!" The Frenchman spoke in his native tongue, but his manner and guttural growling told Cougar what he meant.

She quit struggling just long enough to catch her breath, but he jerked her head against his chest and twisted her arm behind her. She fought to breathe, her face buried against his stinking bulk and his filthy stained muslin shirt. He had galluses holding up his grimy whipcord britches that were tucked into his tall laced hobnail boots. He kicked against her leg and started wrestling her toward the trail. With his bulk and strength, he lifted her off the ground and clomped to the trees. His grip around her neck stifled any cry she could make; it was all she could do to snatch a breath as he lumbered into the trees.

He had been left at the camp with Henri and the young man whose name he could not remember and it was Henri that told him of the trail over the ridge he had used to scout out the village. "It's an old trail, narrow, but it climbs right up that there ridge and you can see the whole village from there!"

"Does it go into the village?" asked Bruno.

"I think so!"

Bruno thought about it a moment, then growled at the youngster, "You! Watch them horses. Me'n Henri are goin' to check out this trail!" He looked at Henri, "Get your lookin' glass!" When he saw the little one had his brass telescope, he motioned to the mousy hanger-on to lead the way and the two mounted the trail to the top of the ridge. Their camp was in the cut between two buttes, the one butte ending in the low ridge that sided the village. Once atop the shoulder of the butte, they could see the trail and the ridge and even the far edge of the camp. Bruno grinned, looked at his little friend, nodded him forward and within moments they were atop the low ridge, bellied down and scoping the camp.

"Find that lodge with the woman!" ordered the big man. Henri knew which woman he wanted and slowly scoped the camp. Most of the activity was after-battle matters, dragging the bodies of the dead Blackfoot to the far trees where they would be buried or disposed, picking up the remains of burnt lodges and more. When Henri saw activity toward the back of the village, he zeroed in and watched. Two women with cradleboards and a toddler were working around a cookfire and he began to grin as he watched.

"I think that's her!" he declared, lowering the scope and looking to his big friend.

"Lemme see!" ordered Bruno, reaching for the brass tube. "Where?" he demanded.

"That big lodge just down from the trees." He pointed to the west edge of the camp. "It's black at the peak and there's two women in front, at the cookfire."

Bruno adjusted the scope, watched the women, then lowered the scope, grinning. "Hehehe, she's the one alright." He looked at the trail before them, followed it as far as he could see, then turned to Henri, "You go back to the camp, case them others come back. If'n he asks, tell him I went after a stray horse, but tie one in the trees this side." His eyes flared and his lip curled as he thought about the woman, "This ain't gonna take long, but I'm gonna enjoy doin' it!"

It was that same trail that he was headed for now

as he dragged the woman along. He stumbled and Cougar twisted in his grip, then buried her teeth in his hairy arm. Bruno always rolled up his sleeves, but now he hollered, "You crazy squaw!" Jerking his arm back, but Cougar would not be denied and bit harder. Bruno released her arm to slap at her to make her loose her bite.

When Cougar felt him release her arm, she twisted away and spat out a chunk of hairy flesh. Bruno looked at his arm, spurting blood and he growled, reaching for her, but she backed away quickly. He had taken her without warning or caution and failed to look for a weapon, the knife that hung between her shoulder blades and she snatched it from its sheath dropping into a crouch, glaring at him as she held the knife loosely to the side.

Bruno's eyes flared as he saw the knife, then he cackled, "Hehehe, ain't you the one. Mighty handy of you to provide the knife that I'm gonna use to cut you to pieces! The only thing we're missin' is that big hound wolf to feed you to, but that's alright, I'm gonna enjoy this anyway." As he talked, he had dropped into a crouch and began circling her, watching her eyes. He had been in many a knife fight and he relished the thought of taking the knife away from her and cutting her like she cut him.

He lunged forward in a feint, but she deftly stepped aside, swiping at his arm. As his right arm still dripped blood, she drew blood with the swipe at his left arm. He jumped back, looking angrily at the cut, then up at her and roared as he charged. But he didn't expect her to kick him in the face a walloping kick, her heel smashing his nose and bringing him erect. He grabbed at his face, eyes squinting, as she screamed her war cry, jumping high and coming down with the side of her foot on his left kneecap, driving it from its socket, and bending his leg backwards. Bruno screamed, as he fell. Before he hit the ground, another kick caught him beneath his chin and her move took her over and behind him.

Bruno rolled to face her, pain shooting through his leg, both arms bleeding, his nose smashed and his jaw probably dislocated if not broken. He glared at her and came to his feet. Totally ignoring his pain and the wounds, he growled like a grizzly and with arms extended, charged headlong at the woman, no concern for the knife or her moves, determined to take her down. He caught her with his shoulder, wrapped his arms around her legs and drove her back, smashing into the tree behind. The big spruce shuddered with the impact, cones and needles falling like a summer storm. Cougar went limp, darkness closing over her eyes, she struggled for air, but none came. She felt herself sliding down the rough bark as she surrendered to the blackness.

Gasping for wind, the big man stumbled to his feet,

glaring down at the woman crumpled at the base of the tree. He staggered back a few steps, saw the knife fallen at her side and bent to pick it up. He wavered as he stood, lip curling and fire blazing in his eyes, "I'm gonna cut you!" he rumbled, but did not move. "You gotta be awake for this, you're gonna watch me make you bleed!" he growled.

***

Even at an all-out run, the wolf and the men following moved more silently than the eagle that glided on the updraft overhead. Every footfall found solid traction, no leaves crumpled, no twig broken, no cones crushed, just the muffled steps that could have passed for a grazing deer. Gabe totally trusted Wolf to find Cougar and he unconsciously checked the load on his rifle as he ran, feeling rather than looking, anything to give the needed assurance. He thought only of Cougar, knowing she was a more than capable warrior and had taken this same man down before, but revenge drives a man to do more than normal, to give no heed to caution, and add determination to purpose. This man was bent on vengeance, but more than that, he had continuously assaulted and killed women wherever he found them and had yet to face any consequences and had no thought of ever being the object of retribution. Such a man is dangerous beyond belief and the man that always vanquished any opponent, paid little attention to regulations and believed himself above and better than anyone, had no reason for restraint.

They were into the trees, following the same trail he used to climb the butte behind the camp and spend time in prayer, but where that trail bent back on itself to climb the hill, Wolf took a lesser trail that pointed into the deeper woods. Gabe missed not a step, long legs bounding through the woods, with only glances of the black form before him, but enough to stay the course. He could not hear, but knew Ezra was behind him, never missing a step nor faltering in his pursuit.

***

Bruno backstepped to a stub of a log, always watching the woman, but her eyelids did not flicker, her breaths coming erratically and no other movement. He sat down, drove the tip of the knife into the wood beside him, then with legs outstretched, he felt his left knee, felt the displaced kneecap and gritted his teeth as he pulled it back into the socket. He spat, shaking his head and stripped his neckerchief from his neck. Using his teeth on one end and his hand on the other, he wrapped the neckerchief tightly around his arm where Cougar had ripped the flesh. He drew it tight, then tied it off. He breathed deep, watching her, waiting for her to come awake. Her lids fluttered and she stirred, took a deep breath and opened her eyes to look around. She started to rise, but Bruno had leaped to her side and put his big boot on her chest and held her down.

"*Non, non, petite femme! D'abord je t'utilise, alors je t'ai coupé!*" said Bruno, grinning wickedly.

Cougar could not understand what he said, but as he waved the knife before him and tugged at his galluses, she had a good idea what he had in mind and she was not going to be his play thing. She tried to twist from under his big boot, but he leaned forward, putting more weight on her chest. She heard a rib pop, fought for breath and her arms flopped to the side. As he lifted his foot, she twisted from under him and tried to rise, but he grabbed a handful of hair and jerked her down.

"Maybe if I cut you up a little, you won't be so hard to handle!" He jerked her hair, pulling her to her knees, her back to him. He started to bring the knife to her throat, but she snapped her head back, hitting him in the crotch and twisted from under him. He lost his grip, and fell to one knee, holding himself as he growled, "I'm just gonna kill you!" he shouted. The tree was behind her and he was before her as she tried to back away, but he fell forward, grasping her buckskin leggings and jerked her feet from under her. She fell to her back, knocking the wind from her lungs and Bruno stood, shaking his head. He watched as she sat up, leaning against the tree.

Bruno stood over her, slowly lifting his hand with the knife, his nostrils flaring, his eyes blazing with anger, his upper lip curling and as he leaned forward slightly. Cougar lifted her arm to block the knife. Her eyes widened, making Bruno think she was showing fear, but the black streak that flew across the small clearing, sailed through the air and teeth closed on the bandaged arm. Bones cracked, Bruno screamed and Wolf bore him to the ground. Wolf shook his head side to side, growling and snarling, ripping flesh and letting blood fly. Bruno grabbed at the massive head, screaming. Wolf was now astride the big man, blood filling the black beard and covering the ground underneath. Bruno reached for Wolf's throat, but the wolf was faster and buried his face in the man's beard, teeth penetrating the filthy matted mass and sinking into the man's throat.

The screams were stifled, the big boots kicked, the massive chest heaved, but the Wolf was the master of this bout. Each shake of his head drove the teeth deeper, slobbers mixed with the blood, snarling and growling prevailed over the grunting and stifled screams. But soon the monster on his back quit moving, but Wolf did not release his grip. A low rumbling growl filled the quiet clearing, until the black wolf stepped back, still astraddle of the man.

Wolf slowly turned to see Gabe cradling Cougar's head against his chest, Ezra standing with his rifle now lowered. Wolf padded to his family, rubbed against Ezra's leg, then dropped to his haunches beside Cougar, felt her hand move through his scruff, then looked up at Gabe. "Good boy, thanks my friend."

23 / VOYAGEURS

The trio started back to the village, Wolf again in the lead but the pace was an easy walk. When they came the Lodge, Dove ran to the arms of Ezra and grabbed at Cougar to include her in the hug. The embrace was warm and welcome, but Gabe broke it up with, "Uh, we," looking at Ezra, "need to go let the rest of the Voyageurs know about their renegade."

Dove looked at Ezra with a question, "But, what . . ."

"If they don't know, they might suspect the Kalispel and no tellin' what they might do. It's best we tell 'em," he explained. The three had talked about it on the way back, having left the body unmoved in the woods. The smells of death and blood were probably already attracting carrion eaters and Gabe and company were unconcerned about the disposition of the body, believing the man had received what he deserved. But if the company wanted to do more, then they could tend to it themselves, but he doubted if they cared enough to go to the trouble.

Gabe spoke to Wolf, "You stay here Wolf, stay with Cougar." Wolf looked up at him, turned and went to Cougar's side and lay down, mouth open, tongue lolling, contentment showing. Both men carried their rifles and each had their over/under Bailes pistol with the rotating barrels in their belts. Gabe also had the two double barreled saddle pistols and he handed one off to Ezra as they walked. "You think they'll want to even the score?" asked Ezra, glancing at his friend.

"If they do, the score's gonna get pretty big in a real hurry. We didn't go lookin' for trouble. That big monster brought it to us, both times. He hadn't counted on Cougar bein' such a fighter, and he sure didn't count on Wolf joinin' in, but . . ."

"Yeah, it's always those 'buts' that make me nervous." He walked a little further, then looked at Gabe, "You want me to side you as we go, or would it be better if I kinda snuck around behind 'em?"

Gabe grinned, "Just side me, but give a little space. You an' that war club need a lotta room!" he declared, looking at the protruding handle of the ironwood war club that hung at Ezra's back. He had fetched it from the gear when they stopped by the lodge, just in case. Ezra had many times proven himself a warrior of the ancients when he handled the war club. He could have been an ancient Mongol, an Oriental

Samurai, or any other of the greats, for he wielded the weapon mercilessly.

The traders were gathering the last of their trade goods together, the pack animals standing tethered nearby as they loaded the peltries and other goods. The expression on Adrien's face told of a good day trading, but when he turned and saw Gabe and Ezra approaching, he sobered and stood, hands hanging loosely at his side as he cocked his head slightly and watched them approach. He could tell by their expression that this was not a friendly visit. He nodded, asked, "You look like a man on a mission. What is it?"

Gabe stopped, stood his rifle on its butt beside his foot, and started, "The big man that you left at the Nez Percé village, did you go back and get him?" Adrien frowned, "Why no! We did not, why do you ask such a thing?"

Gabe glanced at Ezra and slowly shook his head as he looked back at the Frenchman, "Just wonderin' why he was still with your bunch. Seems to me you shoulda left him with the village of Twisted Hair and let them give him what was coming."

"He is a member of this group of Voyageurs," spat Laurent, "and will never be judged by you and never by any Indians! If you had not told Twisted Hair of his little interlude with the woman, he would never have been taken!"

"Interlude? He raped and killed that woman!" de-

clared Gabe, noticing the other three men who had
been busy packing, casually move toward their rifles.
"And you!" pointing to the others, "Stay away from
those rifles!" he ordered, lifting his rifle to hold it,
the muzzle toward them but still at his side. Ezra had
moved away from Gabe a few feet and kept his rifle at
the ready. The other men stopped in place, looking to
Adrien for any sign to start the dance, but the leader
held out an open palm facing them at his side.

Adrien lowered his voice, "That is of no conse-
quence now, the village is behind us and we are leaving here. We will be long gone from this valley very
soon and there is no one to stop us," he explained,
a sardonic smile crossing his face as he cocked one
eyebrow up and put a hand on his hip, a casual and
unconcerned stance.

Gabe said, "Maybe so, but your big man, what was
his name?"

"Bruno," answered Adrien, noticing Gabe's expression 'was.'

"Bruno. Well, Bruno won't be going with you."

Adrien chuckled, "And you think you," grinning
at Gabe and using a tone of derision, "will be man
enough to stop him?"

"Nah, won't need to, you see, when we were at the
camp of Twisted Hair, he attacked my wife and she
cut him up a little, showed him even a woman could
take him down."

Adrien had grown a little tiresome of the exchange and started to turn away, waving his hand as if to dismiss the man as a nuisance.

But Gabe continued, "He tried to take her from our lodge back yonder," nodding his head to the west end of the camp, "and he was able to take her a ways into the trees," he paused, watching the renewed interest of the leader and the other Voyageurs, "but, she done him in again. This time he wasn't shown any mercy. If you're interested, you can find his body in the trees beside that little trail that leads from your camp to the upper end of the village. That is, if there's anything left of it. Scavengers always appreciate a free meal."

Gabe grinned as he watched the anger of the Frenchman rise, his eyes showing white and his nostrils flaring as he clenched his teeth. The muscles at the side of his bearded face tensed as he clenched and unclenched his teeth.

Gaston Durand, the number two man of the bunch, stepped beside Adrien and asked, "You mean he's dead?"

"Better be, otherwise those buzzards will be disappointed!"

"Did he . . ." he glanced to Adrien then back to Gabe, "did he harm your woman?"

"Oh, he tried, and he did hurt her a little, but he was wanting to cut her up and my wolf didn't like that idea."

"You mean your wolf had at him?"

"You might say that. Wolf is a little faster than I am and had he not beat me to it, I would probably done the job a little quicker, maybe just shot him, but it seemed like a reasonable thing for him to be chewed on like that, considering all the native women he cut up and such." Gabe grinned, enjoying himself as he embellished the details just a mite. He could tell the others were wanting to get to their weapons, but he stood his ground. A glance quickly showed several villagers had gathered close by, watching, and listening. The gathering also did not go unnoticed by the traders and Adrien took a few deep breaths, calming himself. He held his hand up to signal his men to stand down, turned around and looked at them and spoke in French, believing no one understood the language, "*Pas maintenant, plus tard,*" he ordered, then turned to look at Gabe with a forced grin.

Gabe laughed, "Not now, later? Really? What makes you think there will be a later, trader?" he looked around at the people that had gathered. The villagers included the chief Bear Track, the shaman Big Canoe and their friend Lame Bull. "These people now know you for who you are and you know you won't get another chance at me or mine, so, you might want to rethink that later business." He intentionally eared back the hammer on his rifle, prompting Ezra to do the same. The click of metal sounded loudly in the moment of tense silence and the Voyageur motioned to his men to finish up.

The Frenchmen quickly completed their packing, carefully picked up their rifles and mounted up to leave. Once mounted, Adrien looked down on Gabe, "No one kills one of my men and does not pay!" he hissed.

Gabe smiled, lifted the muzzle of his rifle, "Would you like to try?"

Adrien huffed, dug heels to his mount and left the village at a canter, packhorses pulling at their leads as the men fought the stubborn animals as they left.

Bear Track stepped near Gabe, "The man that was killed was one of these?"

"Yes, he was the one that killed the woman of the Nez Percé. He had escaped from them and rejoined the traders, but he was left at their camp so he would not be seen. However, he came in over the trail at the end of the ridge and attacked my woman."

"Then what you have done is good," replied the chief, glancing to his shaman and to Lame Bull.

Lame Bull asked, "You said you would be leaving soon?"

"Yes, we will leave at first light." He thought about telling his friend about the agreement made with Thompson to follow the Voyageurs but chose to remain silent. Whatever was to happen did not involve the Kalispel and they had enough to deal with regarding the recent raid by the Blackfoot.

***

When Gabe and Ezra returned to the lodge, the women were anxious to hear about the confrontation and Gabe left the telling to Ezra as he reached for the coffee pot. It had been a long and tiring day and he just wanted to relax and enjoy the coffee and maybe a good meal, the likes of which he could smell coming from the pot at the fire. He smiled, glanced at the boy laying naked on the blanket and playing with a rawhide rattle made by Cougar Woman and leaned back against the willow backrest left behind by Lame Bull. Even with all the challenges, he was enjoying life. He smiled as he looked to the colors of the clouds painted by the retiring sun.

24 / TRAILING

Gabe was belly down; the brass scope stretched out before him as he watched the activity in the camp of the Voyageurs. He had climbed the slope following the trail taken by Bruno when he dragged Cougar from the village, and now lay atop the shoulder of the butte overlooking their camp. He was not surprised to see the remains of the big man picked over by the scavengers and bones scattered about. He knew the voyageurs cared little about the decency of mankind and he fully expected them to ignore the body of the man they had called their friend.

The grey light of early morning was slowly painting the sky off his left shoulder, Wolf lay beside him, head between his paws as he patiently waited. Gabe was focused on the new arrival in the camp. A man had ridden in from the mouth of the draw where their camp lay, slid to the ground as the leader of the Voyageurs approached and animatedly spoke, gesturing back toward the broad valley of the Bitterroot River.

Gabe adjusted the scope to get a clearer image and recognized the man as the little one that had accompanied the big man called Bruno that attacked Cougar. Gabe grunted his disgust as he watched. The men turned to face the mouth of the draw and the little one pointed as he talked. Gabe lifted the scope to the valley, saw on the far side of the river the long bald butte that rose to the taller mountains that were draped in black timber. The little man turned away to his right, gesturing to the south and the Bitterroot River, nodding as he spoke. The leader nodded, put his hand on the little man's shoulder, then turned and barked orders to the rest of the traders. The others scurried around, packing the animals and readying to leave.

Gabe watched for another moment, then looked at Wolf, "Well Wolf, looks like they're leaving, and I'm bettin' they ain't goin' north like they said. I do believe they're headin' out after Thompson and the Northwest boys." He watched, waited and within moments, the entire crew mounted up and led by Adrien Laurent and Gaston, left the camp and at the mouth of the draw, turned south. Gabe retracted the scope as he stood, returned it to the case as he looked at Wolf, "Told ya! They're goin' south!" He shook his head as he started back to camp at a trot.

***

Henri was grinning broadly when he rode back into the camp of the Voyageurs. He was thinking this was going to be his opportunity for some form of revenge for what had happened to his long-time friend and protector, Bruno. He was certain that Adrien would be eager for the news and would go after the Northwest traders and double their take for this journey. That would mean double for his share too. He chuckled at the thought as he slid from his saddle and dropped to the ground.

Adrien saw his scout, the mousy little Henri, ride back into camp and hurried over to hear his report. "You were right!" declared the squeaky scout, "They started north, alright, but up yonder where that river comes in from the east, they crossed over, followed it 'bout a half mile, then turned south." He turned to the mouth of the draw and pointed, "They come down through that brush an' such, then crossed that bald knob of a ridge yonder and dropped down on that side of the Bitterroot and pointed south!" He looked back at Adrien grinning, a self-satisfied smug look on his face. "We gonna go get 'em?"

"Maybe. How far ahead you think they are?" asked Adrien, taking a couple steps toward the bigger valley below, looking at the bald finger ridge that projected into the broader valley, pushing the river to the west side.

"Not more'n a day, after they swung north, they thought they'd hide their trail when they took to the other river there, but they didn't fool me! I knew they had to come out some'ere and come out they did, yessiree!" he chuckled at his report telling what a great tracker he thought himself to be, then added, "But once they turned south, they weren't in no hurry, so, maybe they got, oh, ten miles 'fore dark."

"If that's true, then we could overtake them about mid-day tomorrow," mused Adrien. He turned and started shouting instructions to the rest of the men, then added, "And if you get a move on, we might double our take within a couple days!" The others shouted and hurried their packing, already counting their share of the take and what they would do with the windfall.

***

Wolf reached the lodge before Gabe and Ezra and the women sat beside the cookfire, looking up as he trotted into view. He grinned, nodding and dropped to be seated on the log beside the fire, breathing heavily and working at catching his breath. He looked to Ezra, "Just like we thought. I saw that little one ride into camp, he must be their scout or tracker and from what I could tell, he told them the Northwest boys had turned south." He paused, reaching for the coffee offered by Cougar, "It didn't take 'em long to pack up and start out, going south, just the opposite of what he said they would, probably on the trail of Thompson and company."

Ezra looked at Gabe as he sipped the hot coffee, knowing what he was going to say, but not wanting to hear it, but asked anyway, "So, what're we gonna do?" Gabe thought a moment, then looked around at Ezra and the women, "Well, I can't just sit around and let that bunch of renegade traders get the jump on Thompson, not when I can do somethin' about it! But . . ." and he finished the coffee, tossed the dregs aside and looked around the circle.

"But what?" asked Cougar.

Gabe leaned forward, elbows on his knees as he began, "Goin' south along the Bitterroot, the Northwest boys'll probably be only a day, day and a half, ahead. That means the Hudson Bay bunch could get to 'em real soon like. Now, if . . ." and he began to detail what he had been thinking about pursuit, overtaking the renegades and warning their friends.

"But if we all came," started Cougar, not liking his original suggestion that the women stay in the camp of the Kalispel, "that would put us what, a week away from our cabin?"

Gabe frowned, looked at Ezra and back at the women, "Uh, yeah. Hadn't really thought about that."

Cougar continued, "And then we could be back home and have time to just be at home and lay in supplies for winter, maybe visit with the Salish and even join the fall buffalo hunt." She smiled, glanced at Dove who also smiled, then looked back at the men, waiting for their answer.

Gabe looked at Ezra with his eyebrows raised to suggest a question, but Ezra just grinned, shrugged, and said, "You're the one plannin' ever'thing. You figger it out!"

Gabe looked at the ground, shuffled his feet as he thought, "We'll be movin' kinda fast, and when it gets dark, you'll have to stay in camp. That'll be when we hafta get around the Hudson Bay bunch and get to Thompson, we'll be travelin' by moonlight and there ain't much of it!"

Cougar and Dove both remained a little stoic, knowing there would be more and patiently waited, listening. Gabe continued, "You'll stay in camp till we get back?" he asked.

Cougar looked at Dove who nodded, then turned back to Gabe, "We will."

"Alright then, let's get a move on!" he declared, wondering if what he decided would be the best. But there would be no turning back now!

***

Although he was certain the Northwest company had indeed turned south, Gabe did not want to be too close on the trail after the Hudson Bay bunch. When they left the village of the Kalispel, they rode through the encampment, said their farewells to Bear Track and Lame Bull and took a trail that cut through the trees at river's edge, east of the village. They crossed where a wide sandbar hugged the inside of the big bend and a gravelly bottom showed the shallows and made the crossing easy. Once out of the water, he pointed the group due south toward the bald knob ridge that he remembered the Voyageur leader and his scout had pointed towards.

Less than three miles saw them coming from the dry creek bed and starting over the low saddle crossing over the bald ridge. Gabe lifted a hand to stop, pointed to the tracks before them, then stood in his stirrups and looked to the river valley and motioned them forward. Cougar gigged her roan to move alongside Gabe and his big black, as the trail flanked the tree line that skirted the hillside. She asked, "Is this the trail of Thompson?"

"I believe so. He said they would go south, maybe trade with some of the Salish, even the Shoshone, then the Crow and start back north. He hoped to be rid of the Frenchmen, but . . ." he shrugged. He glanced back at the rising sun that was just off their left shoulder, then back to the trail. "Those tracks," pointing with his chin to the turned soil on the trail, "look to be no more'n a day old, ya reckon?" he said, glancing to Cougar for her thoughts. She was every bit as good a tracker as Gabe and he knew and admired her skill. He watched as she leaned down, her arm at the roan's withers as she lowered herself for a better look. As she pulled herself back erect, she nodded, agreeing.

She looked at Bobcat, already rocked to sleep in his cradleboard that hung before her left knee, held in place by the rawhide thong tied to her saddle frame. The rambling gait of the easy traveling roan was smooth and steady, making it easy for the little one to ride comfortably. She glanced up at Gabe, "Will you just warn Thompson, or will you fight the others?"

"I'm not looking for a fight! I told Thompson I would follow that bunch," nodding across the river, "and try to warn him if they were comin' after him. But I won't run from the fight if I can help it."

Cougar knew her man and knew he would always help a friend or anyone that needed him and if it meant getting involved in a fight, then he would not hesitate, nor would she expect him to, for that was one of the many qualities she loved about her man. Cougar Woman was also a warrior and had been the war leader of her people and led them into many battles, but she had never before encountered a warrior the match of her Spirit Bear. She smiled at the thought, but also realized that no matter the strength and skill of a warrior, there was nothing that could prevent the unforeseeable or the unavoidable and it was the uncertainty that concerned her.

Once over the saddle, the trail hugged the edge of the river, but when the shoulder of the nearby hills crowded, they had to take to the water to make it around the point. Gabe led the way, the steeldust mustang pack horse on the lead line behind him. He had tied the lead for the buckskin mare packhorse behind the steeldust and now trailed both packhorses. He was closely followed by Cougar then Dove on her buckskin with Chipmunk on the saddle before her and the baby in the cradleboard by her leg. Ezra trailed both the Appaloosa mare pack horse and the mule. The shallow water with the gravelly bottom soon gave way to the willow lined bank that had pushed away from the mountain and offered the trail from the water.

When Cougar came back alongside, Gabe nodded off his right shoulder and said, "That's the river that we followed from the Nez Percé village."

She looked back, nodded, then pointing with her chin she said, "There is still lot of snow atop the mountains," looking at the long line of the Bitterroot peaks.

"Yeah, but I don't think it'll be much longer till it's gone, then it'll start all over again."

Cougar smiled, "I like the season of colors the best. The weather is cool, the aspen turn golden, the oak are red and the fresh snow covers the peaks."

Gabe glanced at her, saw the wistful look on her face, then said, "Sounds like you want to go see your family, is that right?"

She smiled, "No, you are my family. You and little Bobcat," she added, reaching down to touch the little one.

Gabe smiled, thinking how good it was to have a family and then thought of what it would be like to have a cabin full of young ones, chuckled to himself and turned his attention back to the trail.

25 / TRAILING

The Northwest men sat around the low burning fire, sipping on their coffee, some of which had a touch of rum added and were enjoying the idle moments before turning in for the night. Two men were already standing guard, and Jacques LaRamee had been assigned the task of scouting their backtrail for any sign of followers. David Thompson sat silent, pondering the route they would take on the return leg of their trade journey.

"Mr. Thompson, sir, I have a question for you." The interruption to the silence came from the youngest of the group, William Ashley. This was his first time out with a company of traders and had handled himself well and proven to be a quick learner.

Thompson looked up at the young man, then glanced around at the others that sat idly by, listening, wondering and watching. "And what might that be?"

replied Thompson.

"Well, I know we're expecting the Hudson's Bay bunch to come upon us and all and I know we're competing companies, but it seems like it's more than competition. I mean, I've heard talk about other companies being attacked, men killed, peltries stolen and such, but . . ."

He let the question hang between them, unable to verbalize his thoughts. He looked up again, "Is there more to it?"

Thompson quietly chuckled to himself, remembering the recent years with the company and the bitter war over trade grounds and fur country. He looked at the young man and began, "Well, I guess you could say things kinda boiled over 'bout a year or so ago. Are you familiar with Rupert's land?"

Ashley frowned, then answered, "I believe so. Isn't that the Hudson's Bay territory, up Canada way? I think it is a big stretch of country from the Bay and west into the mountains, isn't it?"

"That's right. It's been Hudson's territory for more'n a hundred years and they have been very protective of it. When Northwest was formed a few years back, some of the voyageurs with the company wanted to go into Rupert's land and trap, but they were run out or killed, furs taken. So, Simon McTavish, you know who he is?" asked Thompson.

Ashley grinned, "Yeah, he's the top man with the

Northwest company!"

Thompson laughed, "You might say that, but his nephew, William McGillivray is up there too. Anyway, they made a bold move and sent a company north around the Hudson's territory and claimed the Inuit country to the northwest." He smiled at the thought of the name of the company, then continued. "Well, that new country's haul of furs cut into the profit of Hudson's Bay and the word was Northwest's profits were more than double that of Hudson's Bay because of it! Then things got a little nasty and not only that, some of the leaders of our company, Alexander Mackenzie and others, left and started their own, XY company. So, all those things have made the fur business even more cutthroat!"

"But it seems like there's enough for everybody, isn't there?" asked the young man.

"You'd think so, but greed is a poison that kills many a man. Trouble is, the greed from the higher ups kills the men in the field, not the office." Thompson glanced at two of the others, James Frobisher and David Chaboillez, cousins of two of the prominent shareholders of the company.

Frobisher spoke up, "You won't get any argument out of us," nodding toward Chaboillez. "We may be related to some o' them 'higher ups' but not close enough for them to worry about us nor us them!" He glanced at Chaboillez again, "Ain't that right?"

David nodded, "All the good our relation did for us was to get us a job. That's all. I doubt if those in the 'office' would even recognize us if we ran smack dab into 'em!"

The others laughed and Ashley tossed a stick onto the hot coals that flared up just as Jacques LaRamee rode back into camp. He stepped down and accepted the cup of coffee offered by Thompson and dropped the reins of his mount and he sat down on the big rock beside Thompson. Ashley jumped up, "I'll take care of your horse, Jacques!" and led the animal to the picket line with the others.

Thompson waited for Jacques to relax and give his report. After a couple of sips of the hot brew, he began, "I went back about three, four miles. Climbed up on a ridge and scanned the country, but didn't see nothin', didn't smell nothin'. If they're followin' us, they're either further back or they've got a cold camp."

"But what's your gut tellin' you?" asked Thompson, totally trusting in the Métis and his backwoodsman experience.

"That they are back there."

"Yeah," drawled Thompson, staring into the dying coals.

***

The sun was lowering above the Bitterroot peaks, the brilliance almost blinding. It had been a long day with only one short stop for food and rest for the horses. When Gabe pointed the horses to the tree line at the base of the low-rising hills on the east side of the river, everyone relaxed just a mite, knowing rest was coming. The valley had opened wide to the east, but the foothills of the Bitterroots stood like foot sol-diers, guarding the white crowned tops of the royalty known as the Bitterroot range. The many separations between the peaks ended with rock lined gorges that pushed aside steep timbered slopes to mark the mouths of each canyon that carried the spring run-off from the towering mountains.

Gabe slipped to the ground, stood and stretched, bending backwards to pop the bones in his tired back, then stood staring at the majesty of the mountains that bordered the west side of the long valley. He thought of a long line of uniformed soldiers, each one topped with shiny helmets, marching into battle and grinned at his mental image, but nodded as he smiled, thinking *what beautiful country*.

It was a familiar routine, the men stripped the horses of their gear and packs, the women tending the wee ones, then gathering the goods for fixing a meal. Cougar tested the wind, then nodded to Dove to put the fire ring beneath the tall ponderosa that spread long limbs with long needles that would shelter the fire and disperse the smoke. They could not risk being spotted by the company of Hudson's Bay voyageurs and anyone skilled in the ways of the wilderness, could readily see and smell the cookfire. Cougar readied a pot for a stew to be made from the smoked meat and dried vegetables. There had been no thought of fresh meat and would be none, until after the issue with the traders had been settled.

Gabe looked at Ezra as they stacked the packs, "I'm gonna climb that little ridge yonder, see if I can find 'em."

Ezra nodded, knowing exactly who Gabe was looking for and also knowing it would probably be this night that they would have to make the effort to get around the Bay group and warn their friend, Thompson and his men. Ezra watched as Gabe started through the trees, Wolf at his side, rifle in hand and the scope hanging from his shoulder.

As he bellied down, just above the treetops on the face of the ridge, Gabe gave a quick glance to the surrounding land. He was facing to the south on a long finger ridge that pushed into the east edge of the valley of the Bitterroot river. Before him twisted the river in the bottom of the valley that was framed on the west by the towering Bitterroot mountains. With the sun just dropping below the peaks, the cloudy sky was catching the colors of the Master Painter and spreading them across the billowy canvas. Mostly gold, tinged with orange, the bright colors illumined the valley, giving it a wondrous glow, making one think that anything so beautiful could not possibly harbor any evil, but Gabe knew better.

He stretched out the brass tube, put it to his eye and began his methodical scan. He started on the far side, where the shoulders of the big peaks stretched their tunics of black timber, ending abruptly with the long grasses of the valley. He stretched the scope to its full length, slowly moving from landmark to landmark, watching for any movement or smoke, anything that would betray the camp of the Frenchmen. He swung the scope across the valley, then brought his scan along the east side, below their own camp. Nothing.

He lowered the scope, eyeballing the valley with his naked eye, then lifted the scope again. He focused on the river, moving slowly from close in, following the river and moving upstream, searching every cluster of cottonwoods and alder, willows and chokecherry and serviceberry. The river course split, but the water flowed in the east side, the other showing gravel. It was an old riverbed that carried water only in highwater spring runoff. South of the split, the trees grew tall and thick, berry bushes pushing close in and Gabe focused and lingered. There! A thin spiral of smoke, probably from the men putting out the fire before dark, but unwilling to forego their coffee that demanded a fire for broiling meat and brewing the coffee. Gabe grinned, *Gotcha!* With the camp of the Voyageurs spotted, now he had to pick a route to bypass them and make it to the Northwest camp.

Gabe looked down at Wolf, "Well, boy. We got 'em spotted, now it's up to me and Ezra to get the others warned." He rolled to his side, scooted below the crest and stood, then followed Wolf back into their camp.

Ezra asked, "Spot 'em?"

Gabe nodded as he reached for the coffee. He squatted before the fire and sniffed the bubbling stew, "Mmm, that's smellin' good! And I'm so hungry, my belly thinks my throat's been cut!" he declared, grinning at Cougar as she nursed the boy.

Cougar smiled, "We're busy, you'll have to dish up your own."

Gabe chuckled, glanced at Ezra, "Is that how it's gonna be? Once the kids come then we're on our own?"

"What are you complainin' about, you're just number two! I've been demoted to number three already! And not only do I have to help myself, now I've got to take care of Chipmunk, too!"

The women looked at their men, laughing, then looked at each other. Dove said, "Don't you feel so sorry for them?"

Cougar looked at Gabe, then Ezra and back at Dove, who was also nursing and shook her head, smiling, and said, "Not a bit!" Then she looked at Gabe with wrinkles showing between her eyebrows, "Are you going soon?"

Gabe nodded, sipping at his coffee, then explained, "I spotted the camp of the Frenchmen and I'll give 'em time to turn in and be well asleep, then I'll start out."

26 / STEALTH

"The sign's mighty fresh! I'd say no more'n couple hours ahead of us!" declared the mousy scout, Henri. "I smelled their smoke, but I didn't cross the river. Didn't want to be seen an' give 'em a warnin' we was after 'em." He had returned after full dark and had missed the regular meal, but he saw the coffee pot and grabbed a cup to pour him some, glancing back at Adrien. "When we gonna hit 'em, Cap'n?"

Adrien frowned at the little man, even though he was the only one that used the respectful title of Captain. "We'll see, I need to think on it," replied Adrien, non-commitally. He walked away from the smoldering coals, instructed Henri to cover them with dirt before he turned in and walked to the blankets of Gaston where the man sat, cleaning his rifle. Adrien squatted before him, snatched at a long stem of grass and put it in his mouth, biting on the end as he thought. He looked up at Gaston, "Henri says we're only a couple hours behind the Northwest company."

Gaston looked up, did not respond but waited for the man to explain as he continued wiping down his weapon.

"We'll have to hit 'em early on. If we wait till dark, that'll put us so far south, by the time we overtake them and put 'em under, we'll be more'n a week further south, which puts us mighty late getting back to the post."

"Ummhmmm, and the last one in gets the lowest prices for his pelts," added Gaston, laying his rifle aside and picking up his pistol to start cleaning.

"And this valley is wide open, not conducive to a sneak attack," pondered Adrien.

"Umhmm," added Gaston. "But it narrows further south."

Adrien nodded, a slow grin splitting his face, "Yes, it does! And they're staying on the east side of the river. With more timber at the foothills, we might find enough cover in the trees to come closer, maybe even get ahead of them!" He grinned at Gaston, "That's it! We'll get an early start, hang back until we have good cover, then at least get close or ahead and then hit them! Good idea Gaston!" he declared. He stood, starting to leave, then turned back, "Glad you thought of that, it'll make sleeping tonight a lot better! But don't forget to put out guards," he instructed.

Gaston just nodded, then as Adrien turned away, he shook his head, thinking to himself, *Why guards? There are no native villagers near, the Northwest boys are running from us, no need!* He finished his work on his pistol, lay it on his blankets and stood to check on the camp and make a show of posting guards.

"Jean-Phillipe, we need guards posted, so you can take the first couple hours," directed Gaston as he stood by the fire ring. The men had finished their coffee and meal and were just sitting and talking before turning in to their blankets. Jean-Phillipe shook his head and reached for his rifle as he started to rise and Gaston motioned for him to wait. He looked at the others, then said, "Jean-Phillipe will wake his relief, so be ready to take your turn." He spoke to no one in particular, then as the men nodded and rose to turn in, he motioned for Jean-Phillipe to join him as he walked to the edge of the clearing.

He spoke softly as they walked, "Look, I don't think there's any need for a guard, so if you want to bring your blankets and make yourself comfortable, fine. Don't worry about waking the others but keep this to yourself."

Jean-Phillipe grinned, nodding. "I'll go get my blankets now. Thanks Gaston!"

Gaston grinned, waited for Jean-Phillipe to return, then as he settled in, Gaston bid him good-night, but added, "I'll be waking you up, so, don't be nervous and shoot me!"

"Wouldn't dream of it!" answered a happy Jean-Phillipe.

***

Gabe and Ezra worked quickly at making the camp as comfortable as possible, for they would probably need the camp for two or three days. Lean-tos were fashioned with both ground sheets and pine boughs for cover, tied down and made secure with rawhide thongs. A picket line for the animals was stretched at the edge of the clearing at the bottom of the slope of the hill behind them, well-concealed in the taller trees. As they worked, they talked, Ezra asking, "So, 'bout how far behind the Frenchies are we?"

"Oh, couple hours, maybe a little more. But they're on the far side of the river, which will give cover following the trail of Thompson. But, I'm thinkin' it might be just as well for you to stay with the women, take care of them. All I'll be doin' is telling Thompson where the Frenchies are and what they're likely up to, won't take both of us to do that."

Ezra paused, cocked his head to the side as he frowned at his friend, "Worried about Cougar Woman are you?"

Gabe dropped his gaze, working with a rawhide as he answered, "Not just her. There's the young'uns too."

Ezra answered, "You should know by now that Cougar Woman can take care of herself, and so can Dove! And you know as well as I do that a grizzly couldn't get to the kids with them women near."

Gabe looked at the stars overhead, glanced toward the mountains and saw what looked like storm clouds rolling below the peaks, "If that's a storm, we might get a little wet, but it will cover our travelin'." He looked at the scattered stars, saw the crescent of the waxing moon, then added, "Not much light, but should be enough. We won't be in the trees much."

It was just a short while later that the men held their women close, their horses standing ready. Gabe said, "I'm leavin' Wolf with you, to keep you company," he explained.

But Cougar said, "No, he will be better with you." She lifted her eyes to the sky, "He can see better in the dark and he will bring you back to me," she declared, allowing him no argument.

Gabe shook his head, drew her tight and kissed her. The embrace was held by both, but he leaned back, looked at her and smiled, "Be back soon!" Ebony had nudged him just as he was ready to turn, then he swung aboard the anxious horse, smiled at his woman and started into the darkness, Ezra close behind.

The dim light of the moon added to the bright starlight that shone upon the barren slopes on the east edge of the wide valley. The clay hills held little vegetation besides cactus and tufts of bunch grass, typical of the badlands of the Bitterroots. But they shouldered the green of the valley floor that waved tall grasses in the night air. Gabe stayed at the edge of the hills, about three miles west of the river. The chosen route took them between a pair of knobby hills that held scattered scrub piñon and twisted cedar, made so by the lack of water on the dry knobs.

Gabe kicked Ebony up to a canter as they were hidden from the river by the low hills. He remembered when he scoped the valley, these hills were directly opposite or west of the campsite of the Frenchies and they would be well protected from both sight and sound as they traversed the rolling hills.

Believing they were well past the camp of the Frenchies, Gabe saw by the stars they had been on the move for more than a couple hours. He dropped back to a trot then a walk as Ezra came alongside. He pointed to the dark line in the low part of the valley, "The river's yonder, so I reckon we can move a little closer, look for the Northwest camp." He nodded back up the valley, "That storm's movin' this way and that thunder made our travel easy."

"Yeah, it did. But I was wonderin' if we were far enough away from the Frenchies so they wouldn't hear. After all, two horses on the run make considerable noise," added Ezra.

"I think we had some help from on high, what with

the river ripplin', the wind blowin', and the thunder rollin', I don't think anybody woulda heard a couple horses," countered Gabe.

He frowned, reining up, looking at Wolf who stood in his stance, still and watching the darkness. Gabe whispered, "Smell that?"

"Yeah, smoke!" answered Ezra.

Gabe looked at Wolf again, "What is it boy?"

Wolf turned back to look at Gabe, then stared into the darkness where the taller trees lined the river. His focus never wavered, the point about forty to fifty yards before them. Gabe nudged Ebony forward, prompting Wolf to walk ahead. Both men followed slowly and as they neared the trees, the smell of smoke and lathered horses was strong, prompting Gabe to call out, "Hello the camp!"

"Who's there?" came a question from the shadows.

"We're friendly!" answered Gabe. "Just two of us, can we come in?" he asked. With no detectable French accent, Gabe assumed the guard to be one of the Northwest company. He heard some low mumbles, then the voice said, "C'mon in, but keep your hands away from your weapons."

As they came near, Gabe and Ezra held the reins high with one hand and kept the other lifted shoulder high. They could not make out the figure in the shadow that had answered their hail, but the waving muzzle of the rifle motioned them into the clearing where two men holding rifles at the ready waited. Gabe recognized Thompson and said, "David Thompson, it's Gabe Stone and Ezra!"

"Come on in then," declared Thompson, visibly relaxing at the familiar voice.

Thompson reached to the coals with a stick to stir them to life and heat the coffee as Gabe and Ezra stepped down. He looked back at Gabe, down at the Wolf who showed glaring eyes that reflected the glow of the fire, then to Gabe, "Any trouble?"

"No, but they're not far behind you. They're stayin' on the other side of the river, but they're definitely followin' you. My guess is they'll hit sometime tomorrow, or tomorrow night at the latest. There's a storm rollin' down the mountains that might push 'em a little though."

Gabe and Ezra loosened the girths on their horses, let them snatch some mouthfuls of grass and as they held the reins, the men sat on a nearby log. Thompson poured the coffee, then sat back with one of his own. Gabe began, "Have you ever been this way before?" he questioned Thompson.

"No, not in this valley, but east of here. Well, you know, the headwaters of the Missouri, where we met before. I did talk to Bear Track about this country, but . . ."

Gabe nodded, "I scoped out this valley 'fore dark and I think . . ." he started as he began to share his ideas of what the Hudson Bay voyageurs would do and when and where they would attack. He had learned long ago that the best way to plan against an attack, was to put yourself in the position of your enemy and determine what *you* would do if you were the attacker. Then it is much easier to mount a proper defense, or to go on the offense.

The men talked for a couple hours, sketching in the dirt, examining possibilities and probable attacks and more, until they finally arrived at what they considered to be the best possible plan. Since it really was not their fight, Thompson suggested Gabe and Ezra leave the main fight to Thompson and his men, but he asked them to take care of the reserves and the supplies. Gabe and Ezra agreed, stripped their mounts of the gear and went to their blankets for at least a couple hours sleep before daylight.

27 / READY

The first hint of grey light shadowed the eastern hills when the Northwest company started from their camp. Gabe and Ezra rode on either side of Thompson, as Gabe explained, pointing to the mountains on their right that were catching the first morning light on the high snowcapped peaks. "It'll take a couple hours, but I'm sure we can make it. The river splits, a big island in the middle and the wide plain comin' from the two runoff creeks outta the mountains, offer plenty of obstacles for any attack. An' I'm thinkin' that river bed might have some quicksand too."

Thompson shook his head, chuckling, "It'd suit me if the whole bunch of 'em fell into the quicksand and disappeared forever!"

They were following the easy trail on the east side of the river, moving through the tall grasses that grew belly high on the horses. They jumped a bunch of mule deer, all does and spotted fawns that had bedded down near the river, anticipating an early morning drink before traveling back to the hills. The hills pushed in from both sides, narrowing the valley like a funnel crowding everything and everyone closer together when Gabe stood in his stirrups, looked at the Bitterroot mountains and recognized the long ridge, bordered on both sides by deep trench-like gorges and the run-off creeks that bent their courses to the north as they rushed to join the river in the valley below. "That's the place!" declared Gabe, pointing to the west.

A wide alluvial plain that showed eons of deposits from the mountain streams that cut their way through the towering mountains and pushed the mud and silt and gravel into the valley, was now overgrown and lay like a wide sloping fan to carry the small streams into the waiting river. Behind stood the pyramidal peaks, a wide timber-covered stance that stretched to bald granite peaks still clinging to remnants of glaciers in the scars that marked the rugged tips standing well above timberline. While between the taller peaks, a miniature replica fronted the long ridge that separated the deep gorges on either side. And even with the impending fight, Gabe still marveled at the beauty of God's creation.

As agreed, Thompson led the company to cross the Bitterroot river upstream of the fork that formed the island. Gabe and Ezra split from the group and started up the long slope of the alluvial plain that lay before the mountains. Thompson turned his group back to the north along the tree line set back from the west bank of the river. He was a well-traveled man and had known of the perils of quicksand and he grinned as he looked at the wide sandy flats beside the water, sand that had spread wide when the river was high and carrying the spring run-off, but now did little but camouflage the boggy river bottom of black mud that lay beneath.

A gravelly river-bottom that showed under the shallow but clear water invited their crossing and Thompson pushed his mount into the water, leading the men to the island. Maybe eighty yards by a hundred fifty, the island held tall cottonwoods surrounded by a few alders and clusters of berry bushes and willows. The men stepped down, taking their weapons and saddle bags, then ground tying the horses. William Ashley was tasked with tending the horses and had picked out a central thicket of cottonwood that would give ample protection. He started leading the animals, two or three at a time to the central point, tethering each one after loosening the girths and making certain there was graze within reach. Within moments, he had gathered all the animals and began improving the cover. They would be picketed under cover, well away from the fight, watched over by the youngest of the group.

With the old growth cottonwoods, there was ample downed logs and heavy branches the men gathered to improve the breastworks. Driftwood had accumulated at the south end of the island, stacked against the rock formation that split the river and the men robbed the collection of additional pieces to reinforce their cover. It was shy of mid-morning when the men sat back and focused their attention on their weapons. Each had a rifle and pistol, some had more, but each weapon was checked for loads and priming, then powder horns, patches, and balls were lain in a handy place, easily accessed to make reloading as easy and expeditious as possible.

David Thompson had stationed the men about ten yards apart, most on the north and west points of the island. The best marksmen were positioned there, with the others scattered around the remainder of the perimeter. All had good fields of fire with the wide sandy riverbed between them and any attacker. Thompson walked the perimeter, checking with each of the men and carefully looking at every stretch of the river, searching for any giveaways of quicksand.

***

Gabe and Ezra started into the trees atop the wide plain. Rising slowly to the mouth of the canyons that had produced the vast deposit, the point the friends aimed for was the crest of the rise between the two streams, a low rising hillock that would give them a view of the valley bottom. The creek bottom held cottonwoods, but the slope was dotted with juniper and ponderosa with an occasional ash. They stopped in the creek bottom, staying above the rushing muddy water that told of last night's brief storm and tethered their horses on a bit of a shoulder that offered ample graze. Once aground, the men loosened the girths, gathered their weapons and Gabe said, "I'm goin' up there," pointing with his chin as he slipped the case with his Mongol bow from under the fender leather of the saddle. He sat down and strung the bow, using both feet and hands to bend the limbs to nock the string. He stood, hung the quiver from his belt and picked up his rifle and scope case, nodded to Ezra, "Let's go!" and started up the slope.

Wolf walked alongside Gabe, Ezra opposite, as they angled up the rise. As they neared the crest, both men went into a crouch, then to hands and knees before bellying down at the peak. They looked over the valley, searching for movement and Gabe brought out his brass telescope, stretched it out and began his scan. He suspected the Frenchies would cross the river, hoping to come up behind the Northwest company without their crossing being a giveaway, but he searched both banks. Nothing. He lowered the scope, glanced at Ezra then handed off the scope to him.

Gabe rolled to his back, crossed his legs at the ankles and dropped his hand to Wolf's fur and said, "Wake me when they get close."

"Ha! Don't try to kid me, buster! You ain't goin' to sleep," Ezra drawled as he stretched out the scope. He carefully scanned the valley bottom, searching both sides of the river, anticipating seeing the voyageurs any moment, but there was nothing. "I thought they were closer'n this," he said, still moving the scope. There was no response from Gabe and Ezra lowered the scope, looked at his friend and was surprised to see the slow rise and fall of Gabe's chest, believing he was asleep. Ezra then shook his head as he grinned. He whispered, "only you could go to sleep when we're expecting a bunch o' cutthroat renegades to attack at any minute."

"I heard that," replied Gabe, speaking softly and not opening his eyes. The bright sun overhead glared with merciless warmth, but with the dampness of the ground from the previous nights brief storm, the warmth was a welcome respite.

Ezra turned his attention back to the scope and slowly moved it along the bank of the river, then startled, he jerked back. A big moose had jumped from the backwater at a bend of the river and started to the trees at an all-out run. He had been spooked and Ezra adjusted the scope, searching for the cause of the moose's alarm. Then he saw them, the band of voyageurs, strung out in a double line, trailing the pack horses and he began to count, "Looks like there's six or seven of 'em, and they got 'bout that many packhorses, maybe more."

Gabe rolled to his belly, looking in the distance, hand shading his eyes. Ezra handed him the scope and he focused in on the group. "Ummhmm, that's the blackguard called Adrien in the lead. Don't see the little 'un, prob'ly scoutin' the other side. Wait a minute, here comes their scout." Gabe continued watching as the little man made his report, gesticulating upstream toward the narrowing of the valley. Then the leader shouted some orders, motioning to the trees on the west side of the river and the band turned to take the packhorses into the trees.

Gabe grinned, "They're gettin' ready, leaving the pack string in the trees, probably with one or two of the bunch." He watched, waiting until he saw the men checking their weapons, pulling the rifles from the scabbards and sheaths, checking the loads. He handed the scope to Ezra, "Well, here goes. Gonna warn Thompson." He stood, nocking one of the whistling arrows, and with the jade thumb ring, he brought the weapon to full draw, elevated the aim and loosed the long black arrow with the bone whistle. It arched high and disappeared against the bright blue of the sky as it began its whistling descent. Gabe had calculated they were about four hundred plus yards from the point of the island, but also about a hundred feet higher and he was certain the arrow was on target. The agreed upon signal was that Gabe would send an arrow to alight on the side of the island where he expected the force of attackers to strike.

***

"What the blazes?" asked Jacques LaRamee as he looked up into the glare of the sky. The whistling was unlike anything he had heard before and knew there was not a bird in the mountains that could make that long of a screech. The whistle increased to a high-pitched squeal, then the arrow plummeted to impale itself in a wet log at the hastily made breastworks of the island. The thunk startled those nearby and Thompson ran to look. He was amazed at what he saw, knowing the approximate location of the two men high up on the slope above the river. He turned to the others, "Alright men, the Hudson's Bay boys are comin' an' they're hittin' this side first. Pick your shots, but stagger 'em, don't want ever'body shootin' and then no one with a loaded weapon. I'll take the first shot!"

He looked from one to the other, each giving a nod of assent, then turning back to watch. These were men that had been bloodied in battle before, all but Ashley and Thompson was confident in each man doing his job. But he also knew that shooting at white men was different that defending yourself against an attacking and screaming Indian, but his men knew the Frenchies not only wanted their plews and packs, they wanted their lives and would leave no one behind to tell the story. Thompson heard the clicks of hammers being eared back and went to his place to pick up his rifle and be ready.

28 / BATTLE

Gabe and Ezra sat below the crest of the rise, shielded by the treetops below them and watched as the band of voyageurs rode toward the waiting Northwest band. The leader lifted a hand to stop them, then motioned to the island beyond the low trees at river's edge. He turned to his number two man, pointed to the far side of the river and waited while he and two of the men slowly crossed the shallow waters to approach from the opposite shore. Once he saw they were in place, he motioned both groups forward.

Gabe glanced at Ezra, "I think he's figgered out they're on the island. He split his bunch. Right smart of him." He watched a moment, then turned to Ezra, "How 'bout you goin' back up yonder and takin' care of those two young pups they left behind with the packhorses. I'm gonna come up behind these turncoats and help out Thompson."

"What'chu think I should do with the young'uns?"

"That's up to you and whatever they do. Mebbe send 'em home, if they got one," answered Gabe as he started into the trees to fetch Ebony, Wolf at his side.

"Their mommas prob'ly don't want 'em back!" suggested Ezra, following his friend.

***

Adrien started through the trees, stopping at the edge of the tree line and peering through the thicket at the breastworks piled at the perimeter of the island. He saw three, four rifle barrels and knew they were waiting for his attack. He nudged his horse forward a few steps, pushing aside the branches of the scraggly juniper. He hollered, "Hello the island! This is Adrien Laurent of the Hudson Bay company!"

An answering shout came from Thompson on the island, "I know who you are! And you know who we are. I also know what you want, so get on with it!"

"O mon amie! We do not want to fight you! We just want your peltries, those that you stole from the Kalispel and others. The pelts that are rightfully ours!"

"How do you figger they're yours?" answered Thompson, watching the trees closely. He bent to the side and spoke quietly to Jacques LaRamee, "Move over to the far side, I think he split his forces and biding his time till they hit us."

LaRamee nodded, motioned to Dumont to join him and the two squirreled their way to the far side, their movements hidden by the piled-up driftwood and downed cottonwood logs. He glanced back at Thompson and nodded, then turned to peer through the stack for any movement.

Adrien answered Thompson's question, "Because all this territory is the land of the Hudson Bay. You are interlopers!"

"This ain't Hudson territory! I do believe you are lost Laurent. Maybe you should go home and try again!"

"But monsieur, those pelts are not worth your lives! We will wait while you mount up and leave and leave the pelts behind. That way, you will live, we'll be happy and no one dies!"

"You plannin' on talkin' me to death, Laurent?" asked Thompson.

The answer came when Laurent nodded and the rifle of Bernard Moreau roared. The man had taken careful aim at a point just behind an extended rifle barrel, believing he could hit the man behind. But the bullet ripped a groove in the grey cottonwood log and tore off a chunk of bark, injuring no one. At the shot, Thompson ducked below the breastwork but hollered at his men, "Hold your fire!"

At the sound of the first shot, Gaston Durand and the two men with him, Henri Petit and the young man, Claude Marchand, slapped legs to their horses and lunged into the shallow water to charge the east side of the island. Water splattered, splashing high and the men held their rifles close to their chest to keep them dry. Durand was in the lead and dropped the muzzle of his rifle to fire one-handed, but the uneven river bottom caused his horse to stumble just as he pulled the trigger and the shot went wild.

Jacques LaRamee waited just a breath before he squeezed off his shot. The bullet from the leader of the charge whipped through the leaves above his head and when the horse gained solid ground, LaRamee fired, the bullet smashing into the upper chest of Durand, driving him backwards off his mount. He tumbled end over end and landed on the back of his head, breaking his neck, but he was already dead from the .54 caliber bullet.

Henri Petit held back as Durand started the charge and saw him take the bullet. Henri, ever the back-shooting coward, jerked hard on the reins, pulling his horse's head around and turned back to the trees. As he turned, he saw the young man, Claude, fly head first off his mount that had sunken into the boggy sand at river's edge. The sudden stop and plunge into the deep mud sent the young man flying. Henri saw him splash into the same mud, but didn't wait to see what happened, digging his heels into his horse's ribs to leave the fight and find safety. He grinned as he thought of another way to get his vengeance on his friend's killers.

LaRamee saw the rider to the left turn tail and hit the trees and out of the corner of his eye he saw the young voyageur take his spill, but the splashing water and mud obscured him from view for a moment. When he saw the leader of the charge was dead, LaRamee turned his attention to the boy in the water, but saw the horse sinking, only its head above water now and there was no sign of the boy. LaRamee twisted around to look both upstream and down, but there was nothing. He shook his head, knowing the mud bog or quicksand had claimed both horse and rider. With no other threats, he looked back to where the others were partially obscured in a cloud of powder smoke.

LaRamee motioned to Dumont and the two dropped into a crouch and joined Thompson and the others. He dropped behind the logs to reload and Dumont peeked over the edge and lifted his rifle to take aim. There was a body floating face down and snagged on a rocky sandbar, but smoke came from the trees where others were shooting.

∗

Laurent hollered at Bernard Moreau, "I'm hit! You alright?"

"Yeah, they came close, but haven't hit me!"

"But I could take you both real easy," came a growling voice from behind them. Laurent turned back and saw the tall blonde mountain man that killed Bruno, standing with his rifle aimed right at Laurent's belly.

"Easy mon amie, you could hurt someone with that!" answered Adrien, glancing at Moreau who had turned his head, but his rifle was pointed toward the island. It was obvious that the tall man had seen both of them, but did he know about the others? Laurent added, "It would be best if you just lay your rifle down before my friends come through those trees. They would think you mean to harm me and, well, we wouldn't want anything like that to happen, would we?"

Gabe grinned, "You are all that's left. Your friends over there," nodding to the far side of the river where Durand and the others had gone, "are done for and they're not coming back. Now, if you want to see another sunrise, then lift your hands high and very carefully step away from your rifles."

Adrien glanced at Moreau and gave a slight nod, bent to lay his rifle down then lifted his hands high and took a step toward Gabe. Moreau watched and as Laurent bent to drop his rifle, he spun with his in hand, cocking the hammer as he spun, seeing Laurent start to reach for his rifle but before Moreau could complete his move, he saw nothing but teeth as Wolf lunged, mouth wide and buried his teeth in the man's face, driving him to the ground. The rifle fired, but the shot went high into the trees as Moreau tried to scream, but when his back hit the ground, Wolf had ripped most of his face away. Then the wolf went for the throat, ripping and snarling, digging with his hind feet into the man's legs and clawing with his forelegs, tearing the man apart.

The attack by the wolf startled Adrien and he snatched up his rifle and lifted it toward Gabe, but the big Ferguson rifle roared and bucked and the heavy lead ball drove into Adrien's chest, driving at an angle to rip apart his lungs and more as it exited just below the opposite shoulder blade, taking a chunk of bone and flesh with it. Adrien's eyes flared, his lips snarled in protest, but no sound came as he crumpled in death, face hitting the dirt before him.

Gabe called, "Wolf!" and the big black and now bloody beast came to his side, head swinging side to side looking for any other threat to his pack leader. He dropped to his haunches beside Gabe then as Gabe started toward the edge of the trees, he walked beside him. Gabe lifted his voice, "Thompson! It's Gabe Stone! These are all dead! You alright?" he hollered.

"Yeah! Come on over!" answered a very relieved Thompson. He stood to see Gabe push through the trees and stand at the edge of the river bank, grinning.

"Where's your friend?" called Thompson.

"He went to check on any others that might be left behind with their packhorses," answered Gabe as he stepped into the shallow water. With his rifle held high, he waded across the gravelly bottomed river, Wolf at his side. He looked down to see Wolf duck his head under and then roll in the water to rid himself of the blood of battle and both stepped to the bank. Wolf rolling his coat and shaking the water free and onto his friend, who shook his head, laughing.

Gabe looked up at Thompson, "Any losses?"

"None! They thought they'd take us from the other side, but Jacques here put a stop to that!" replied Thompson.

Jacques chimed in, "Actually, we just took one man. One turned tail and ran off, the other one and his horse, disappeared in the quicksand," nodding to the far side.

Both Gabe and Thompson frowned, shaking their heads and Thompson said, "That's a hard way to go!"

29 / GUARD

Ezra went up the draw until there were enough trees to provide cover, then rode over the low-rise ridge and worked his way to the long draw that carried the run-off stream from the northernmost canyon. The twisted scar that marked the wide alluvial plain was heavily timbered with stunted cottonwoods, alders, willows and more. Deeper than the one they had used for cover when they scoped out the approach of the voyageurs, this draw was more of a ravine, with steep sides and a wide bottom. But the copses of trees and more offered ample cover for Ezra's approach.

He rode high on the timbered slope, then dropped into the wider part of the draw and tethered his horse. Slipping the Lancaster rifle from its sheath, he checked the load and priming, then drew the pistol from his belt and checked it. He was over a hundred yards from where he believed the packhorses and their guards were picketed and slowly began his approach. Ezra was as skilled as any native and more than most, moving through the trees and brush as quiet as the stealthiest of God's creatures.

He smelled the horses and dropped into a crouch, searching the coverts for movement. Then the flick of a horse's tail caught his attention and he searched for the guards. He knew those that were left behind were usually the youngest and less trusted in a fight, but still he took no chances. As slow as a tired turtle, he moved to the side, looking for the man or men. Finally movement at the far edge of the picket betrayed the presence of a young man. But Ezra knew there could be at least one more and he moved again to see the rest of the clearing. But there was no one. As he watched, the young man stood, his back to Ezra and stretched, then bent down and picked up a stick and tossed it toward the creek. The small stream chuckled over the rocks, the sound of the cascades masking any noise that Ezra would make, then carried the thrown stick downstream.

Ezra slowly moved closer, the butt of his rifle at his shoulder, the muzzle pointed down, and he stopped about fifteen feet behind the young man. With another quick look around for anyone else, Ezra said, "Don't move!" But the young man was startled and quickly turned, a pistol in his hand.

Ezra heard the hammer cock as the man turned

and lifted his rifle. Both weapons fired almost at the same time, the bullet from the pistol whistling past Ezra's ear, but the one from the rifle taking the young man high on his right chest, driving him to the ground. Ezra dropped his rifle and snatched his pistol from his belt as he ran to the boy's side. He was still alive, scared eyes looking up at Ezra. The pistol had fallen from his grasp and the boy's hand covered the wound at his chest. He looked at Ezra, "You shot me!"

Ezra frowned, "You shot at me too."

"I didn't mean to, you scared me." Ezra knelt beside the boy, lifted his head and pulled it to his lap, shaking his head as he saw the boy was probably no more than fourteen or fifteen years old. The boy tried to look at his wound but struggled and couldn't see it. He looked up at Ezra and asked, "Am . . . am I gonna die?"

Ezra thought the boy spoke without a French accent and wondered why he was with the French but discarded the thought as he sought an answer. "I dunno boy. What's your name?"

"Matthew, Matthew Higgins." He struggled for breath, "Gonna break my momma's heart." He looked up at Ezra, "She's been prayin' for me. Told me many times I needed to get things right with God, but I wouldn't listen. Now . . ." his eyes fluttered, and he fought to look around him.

"We can do that now, if you want," answered Ezra. "My Pa's a preacher and I could help you."

"Can you? Really?" he asked, squirming for relief from the pain.

"Yes. Let me tell you . . ." and Ezra began explaining to the boy how Jesus loved him, loved him so much He went to the cross to die for him.

"But why? Why would he do that for me? I'm no good!" answered the boy, weakly.

"Here's what you need to know, *all* of us are sinners, that's what it says in Romans 3:23, and because were 'no good' as you say, there's a penalty for that sin and that's death and hell forever, Romans 6:23 says that."

"Yeah, I've heard that before," mumbled the boy.

"But there's more. Even though we're sinners, God still loves us and he loves us so much, he sent his son, Jesus, to die on the cross to pay the price for our sins, so we wouldn't have to, that's in Romans 5:12 and 6:23." Ezra paused, looking in the boy's eyes with compassion and continued. "And when He paid that price for us, He bought the gift of eternal life for us, but it's a gift like any other, it has to be received."

"Ho ... how do I do that? That's what my momma wanted me to do," answered the boy, struggling to breathe.

"Simple. Just ask in prayer. Now, I'm gonna pray and when I do, I'll say a prayer like you need to and if you mean it with all your heart, not just to try and escape death, but you really want that free gift of eternal life, then you pray with me. Understand?"

"Yeah, I understand. That's what my momma wanted and that's what I want," answered Matthew.

Ezra nodded and started praying. "Dear Lord, we come to you in need. Matthew here is hurt bad, but he knows he needs Jesus and Lord, we want to ask for that." He paused, looked at the boy, then continued, "Now Matthew, if you mean it, then just repeat this after me, but only if you really mean it. Dear God, I want to trust you today to take me to Heaven when I die. Forgive me of my sins and come into my heart and give me that free gift of eternal life. Let Jesus be my savior. In His name we pray, Amen."

Ezra heard Matthew repeat the prayer, one phrase at a time and as he said Amen, he heard the boy choke a little and Ezra looked up at a smiling young man, who nodded his head to Ezra. Then he struggled for a breath, his eyes widened and he fell limp in Ezra's arms, dead. Ezra slowly shook his head and lowered the boy to the ground. He stood, looking around and saw no evidence of any others, then went to the stacked packs and rummaged around until he found a shovel. He glanced back at the boy's body, then went to the edge of the trees and started digging a grave.

Ezra had heard the sounds of gunfire as the battle raged below, but that was at least a couple miles away and he was not concerned. He finished the digging, placed the boy's body in the grave and stood to say a prayer. He thanked the Lord for the opportunity given in the last moments of the boy's life and with another look at the young man, filled in the grave and gathered some rocks to cover it over, knowing it was but a feeble effort to keep the scavengers away, but also realizing they would probably try to get at the body anyway. He stood, looked at the papers he had taken from the boy's pockets and looked at the letter that was in the handwriting of a woman and the address was in Philadelphia, Ezra's own hometown. He shook his head, stuffed the envelope in his pocket and started into the trees to fetch his horse.

He returned to the packhorses just in time to see Gabe riding up, rifle across the bow of his saddle, searching the trees for anyone. Ezra hailed him, "C'mon in Gabe, no danger!" and watched as his friend and Wolf trotted into the clearing.

Gabe glanced around, "What, no one here?"

"Oh no, there was one," answered Ezra, nodding to the grave at the far edge of the clearing.

"Oh," Gabe replied, glancing at the expression on Ezra's face, then stepped down. He looked at his friend, "Problem?"

"He had his back to me, I told him not to move, but he turned and had a pistol, fired it at me as I shot him. But," explained Ezra, then dropped his eyes to the ground, "he was just a boy, maybe fifteen or so, and said he didn't mean to and that his momma would be broken hearted."

Ezra shook his head as he looked at the grave, then back at Gabe, "But, when he said his momma wanted him to get right with Jesus, I helped him get that done."

Ezra nodded, reached out and put his hand on Ezra's shoulder, "That's the best thing you could have done, my friend. Sometimes God has to do some pretty drastic things just to get somebody's attention. It's not your fault."

"Yeah, but, that doesn't make it hurt any less. But I reckon, time will take care of that, hopefully. Time and some talkin' with the Lord," surmised Ezra. He turned and motioned to the valley, "I assume the Northwest bunch won out?"

"You could say that. I told 'em we'd bring the pack-horses down to 'em 'fore we go back to our camp," explained Gabe.

Ezra nodded, lifted his rifle to replace it in the sheath at his saddle, then went to the packs and began to pack up the animals. It was not an easy job, bundles of pelts are heavy and difficult to maneuver onto the pack saddles, but the two men soon had everything packed and tied down and started back to the Northwest crew at the island.

Thompson and company had crossed the river, pack horses in tow and were on the flat beside the river when Gabe and Ezra approached. The pack string of the Hudson Bay company numbered eight animals, all well packed and Thompson grinned at the bounty. He looked at Gabe and Ezra, "I think you fellas need your pick of the packs and animals to improve your supply, what say?"

Gabe grinned, nodded to Ezra, and said, "Sounds good to me!" It didn't take long for the company and Gabe and Ezra to sort out a couple panniers full of supplies including several pounds of coffee, flour, sugar and more. The grinning duo waved goodbye to their friends and started across the river, pack horse trailing and turned north to their camp and their families.

30 / REVENGE

It would be all of a day's travel to get back to the camp with the women and the day was almost gone. Off their left shoulder, the sun was lowering to its resting place among the peaks of the Bitterroot range, leaving just a few hours of daylight travel for the men. They were backtracking the same route they traveled after they joined Thompson and Gabe noticed something that bothered him and reined up to step down for a closer look. He dropped to one knee, reaching down to closely examine the tracks before him. He looked up at Ezra and pointing to the tracks, "See this?"

Ezra leaned down for a closer look, glanced at Gabe, still on his knee, "Somebody's goin' back the way we came." He referenced a single set of tracks that were going north but following the same trail.

"I've seen these tracks before, they were with the Hudson Bay bunch. But I'm not sure who they belong too," stated Gabe.

Ezra huffed, "Obviously the one that ran away! Remember what you said that LaRamee said about one of 'em turnin' tail and runnin' off. He said it was the little one, the one we knew was their scout. And he's the same one that was buddies with the big 'un you killed back in the woods, yonder," nodding downstream toward the distant Kalispel camp.

"Yeah, I think you're right. But he couldn't know we were with the Northwest boys, could he?" asked Gabe as he stuck his foot in the stirrup to swing back upon Ebony.

Ezra shrugged, "If he's a good tracker and they followed us through the canyon when we left the Nez Percé, then when he came across these tracks," motioning to their tracks before they joined the Northwest company, "he might have guessed we joined 'em."

"I don't like that," declared a somber Gabe. Both men knew what that foretold, for if the scout from the voyageurs was backtracking them, it was for the sole purpose of finding their camp and their women. And there was no telling what a blackguard like him might have in mind, especially since he knew it was Gabe and Cougar that were responsible for the death of his friend, Bruno.

Gabe glanced at Ezra, then kicked Ebony into a canter knowing Ezra would not be left behind. The packhorse stretched out as the lead grew taut when

Ebony kicked up the pace, but the big grey packhorse was game and quickly matched Ebony stride for stride. After a short while, Gabe drew Ebony down to a walk, letting him get a breather and he glanced over at Ezra, "We'll keep movin' through dusk, but when it falls dark, we'll stop and give the horses a chance to rest up a bit, get us somethin' to eat, but I reckon we need to push through the night. That little weasel has what, three, four hours head start on us, doesn't he?"

"Yeah, reckon you're right, although I wasn't down there when things busted open, but three to four hours seems about right," answered Ezra. His mind was as much on Dove and the little ones as was Gabe's on Cougar and their newborn. A vengeful, vindictive and probably a little on the demented side, little snake like the man they believed they followed, was capable of anything and would stop at nothing to get his vengeance. Both men knew their women were more than capable and either one would be a match for the little man, but the children were also in danger and the women would seek to protect them at all costs. Both men stared into the waning light as they rode, minds and hearts in turmoil.

True to their plan, once the sun had finished its paint show of the evening and dropped below the mountains, dusk soon faded and as the darkness lowered its curtain, the men drew up beside a small creek and slid from their saddles. They stripped off the saddles and gear, rubbed the horses down with handfuls of grass and let them roll then walk to the stream for some water. The horses snatched clumps of grass as the men stretched out to munch on some jerky. They were not interested in a full meal, nor were they willing to take the time and effort to brew some coffee. Their thoughts were on their families and they were restless, sitting up, lying back, standing and walking, but neither man willing to voice their thoughts nor their fears.

It was Wolf that stirred the men to action, he had nudged Gabe as he sat at the creek bank chucking stones into the water, then trotted toward the horses. Gabe looked at Wolf, then saw all three horses, standing side by side looking at the men as if to say, "Come on, let's go!" Gabe glanced at Ezra, "Looks to me like they're ready to go, you?"

Without a reply, Ezra jumped to his feet and went to the gear to start saddling his big bay. Within moments, they were on the trail again and Ezra was the first to kick his bay to a canter. They set the pace with canter, walk, canter, walk, always giving the horses their heads and letting them set the pattern. Ebony quickly showed he was anxious and eager for the trail and with head high, long mane and tail flying in the wind, he stretched out and set the overall pace for the group.

The moon was waxing toward full but was only showing half. Yet the clear night offered starlight and moonlight, clear trail and cool breezes in their face. They were making good time and both men, though not voicing the thought, were hoping the voyageur scout would stop for the night while they kept on the move. But a scripture verse came to Gabe's mind, James 1:8 *A double-minded man is unstable in all his ways.* He shook his head, and thought it was a reminder from the Lord of the wickedness and instability of the man they pursued. He sucked a deep breath, trying to calm himself, but it was of little use. Then he remembered something, glanced at Ezra and reined up to talk.

"When we came from the camp, we swung wide, moved to the east to keep from bein' heard by the Frenchies. That took us a longer way, but if we go straight, instead of up and around those knobs," pointing with his chin to the series of low hills that bore timber and stood as shadows off to their right, "we will save some miles and time!"

Ezra nodded, "Then lead the way!" and pointed to the flat and rolling grassland before them. Gabe nodded, slapped legs to the big black and started off at a canter. He hollered down to Wolf, pointing ahead, "Go boy, scout it out!" and the big wolf stretched out, long leaping strides widening the distance between them. Gabe glanced above his right shoulder at the half moon, showing bright but with a hint of a halo, guessing the time to be just past midnight. They still had a long way to go.

Ebony slowed to a walk, already accustomed to the rhythm of the pace from canter to walk to canter. He bobbed his head, ribs expanding as he gulped deep breaths, never faltering in his step. Ezra was beside Gabe, often glancing to his friend, "Think we're gonna make it?"

"Oh, we'll make it, but will we be in time? I dunno," answered an exasperated Gabe, frustration and impatience showing as the moonlight shadowed his face.

Again, Ebony stretched out to his rocking gait of a canter, Gabe moving easily with the smooth motion. Images of Cougar came to his mind, the image of her cowering on the ground at the feet of the big monster Bruno, his hand lifted high, the blade of the knife glimmering in the speckled sunlight that came through the trees. Her eyes showed a blend of fury, anger and fear as she fought to free her arms from the ham hock mitts of her crazed attacker and only the lunging form of Wolf spared her. Gabe shook his head to free his mind of the image and the thought that it could happen again.

They came to a narrow brush shrouded creek and pushed through the thickets, to cross the shallow stream. Gabe glanced left and right, recognizing the creek as they came from the water, to their left was the Bitterroot river and beyond that, the mountains rose as dark specters of night, the moon painting shadows on their flanks. To their right across the grassy flats lay the barren badlands that shouldered the low mountains, devoid of any remnant of snow. He looked at Ezra, "We're close! Those," pointing before them, "are the trees and hills where our camp lies." They rounded the point of a long low ridge that pointed to the eastern hills, the valley opening wide before them. Less than a mile away were the timbered hills they sought.

"I remember! Didn't we go thataway," pointing to his right, "and cross this same ridge yonder?" answered Ezra.

"That's right. I think we've cut some time off, but . . ." As he spoke he reined Ebony toward the trail they had taken from the camp. When the tracks showed themselves as dark turned soil, Gabe reined up and dropped down. He made a quick search, saw what he dreaded, then swung back onto Ebony, "He's been here!" referring to the tracks of the voyageur scout. Gabe pointed toward the hills and dug heels to the stallion's ribs. Ebony lunged forward, almost unseating his rider, as he stretched out, head low and began to run.

Gabe knew his stallion loved to run and both he and the horse felt the urgency of the moment. Gabe lay low on Ebony's neck, the long black mane slapping his face and the tail lifted like a battle flag on a pirate's galleon. Earlier, Gabe had thrown the lead of the packhorse over the animal's neck and let him follow at his own pace and the big grey kept pace with the stallion, less than half a length behind. Ezra was on Gabe's right, also leaning well over the neck of his bay.

They were nearing the timbered ridges when Ebony slowed his pace and Gabe sat erect. Something was in the middle of the trail and they reined up, approaching cautiously. As they neared, a quick glance showed a dead horse, with saddle and tack still bound, lather showing at the edge of the saddle, beneath the martingale, at the tail and neck. A fine wisp of steam rose from the lathered neck, the body still warm. Lifeless eyes wide open, mouth wide as the animal had fought for air before dying. The horse had been mercilessly run to death, dying with its last step and breath spent to please its crazed rider.

Gabe glanced at Ezra, both men shook their heads as they reined around the carcass. With a quick glance to the trail and the trees beyond, Gabe said, "He's afoot, and that makes him even more dangerous. Let's go to the trees, then we'll follow on foot."

"It'll be hard to track in the darkness, especially in the trees. I'm goin' on into camp, just in case he ain't made it there yet. You can follow him if you want!" declared Ezra, nudging his bay toward the trail by the trees. Gabe motioned to Wolf and the two started to the trees.

31 / VENGEANCE

When Gaston Durand charged across the river ahead
of Henri Petit, the little man pulled back on his
mount, moving slightly behind the bigger man, using
him as a shield. But when the breastwork blossomed
with powder smoke and lead, Henri did not hesitate
to jerk the head of his horse around and retreat to
the trees. As he turned, he saw the young man that
rode with them take a header off his mount that had
bogged down in the quicksand. But Henri was only
concerned about himself and he sought the safety of
the dark timber.

A bullet whistled past, making Henri drop low and
dig his heels into the ribs of his mount, driving hard
into the trees. Rifle fire racketed through the woods,
echoing across the river and Henri knew he wanted
away from here. He stopped his horse at the edge of
the trees, leaning down to look to the flats beyond,

then a glance to his left revealed a mounted figure coming from the hillside, a familiar figure. He waited just long enough to recognize the blonde buckskin clad mountain man that was the one who killed Bruno. It was *his* woman that enticed his friend to his death and now that man was here, coming to the aid of the Northwest bunch. But, if he was here, where was his woman?

Henri chuckled, thinking, *Surely she is not with him. He probably left her behind with the other woman. Yeah, they had kids and would stay behind.* He cackled to himself, waited until the man disappeared into the woods, then gigged his mount from the trees. He would look for their tracks and back track them, it would be easy!

And it was easy. He spotted the churned soil made by the band as they came from the flats. He kicked his mount to a run, he needed to get away from here and he could follow that trail left by maybe twenty horses easily. When he thought he was far enough away from the island and the gunfire had slackened, he reined up and dropped to the ground, going to one knee to examine the tracks carefully. Any skilled tracker can pick out the tracks of individual horses, for they are as unique as the prints on a man's hand. A nick here and notch there, maybe one hoof toed in a mite, many different ways to identify them and once known, they are remembered. He saw two sets of familiar tracks, tracks he had seen and followed beside the river in the canyon when they came from the camp of the Nez Percé. He nodded, grinning and began thinking about what he would do when he found their camp.

He stepped back aboard his bay gelding, kicked it up to a canter and began following the trail. When dusk dropped its long shadows, he saw the trail split. Coming from his right and away from the river were the familiar tracks he followed. He stopped, looked down and read the sign, *The Northwest bunch came along here, and those two came from yonder. They're the ones I want to follow.* He cackled audibly as he pointed his mount to the lesser trail.

He pushed on through the night, the only time he slowed or stopped was when they came to a creek or mountain stream and he let his horse get a drink as he bellied down and put his face in the water to drink and refresh, coming wider awake with every dunking. The further he rode, the more he imagined what he would do and the more anxious he became. He was merciless with his horse, caring nothing about the animal and focused only on his anticipated revenge.

It was after midnight when he grew tired, struggling to stay in the saddle and finally reined up to get some rest. The little stream chuckled over the rocks and under the overhanging willows as he stretched out with the long rein wrapped around his wrist. The horse drank his fill, and cropped the grass, then stood hipshot, dozing in the dark early morning.

A long lonesome howl of a coyote jerked both horse and rider awake and the little man stood, stretched, then grabbed the last of his jerky from his saddle bags and tightened the girth before stepping aboard the tired mount. He gigged the bay to take the trail and the vengeful man was once again bound for his intended prey.

The bay slowed to a walk, still following the trail of the two riders made the day before, but as he climbed the low ridge, the animal stumbled, caught himself and struggled up the small incline. Henri Petit had been dozing, head bobbing with the gait of the horse, until he stumbled, then he came awake, unconsciously grabbing the pommel to stay aboard. He cursed the animal, looked into the moonlit flats and saw the rise of other hills before him. He lifted his eyes to the moon, now lowering in the west, and guessed it to be early morning, just before first light.

As they came from the ridge, the trail led across the flat toward the slopes before him, and the bay gelding, now covered with lather and head hanging, stumbled again, lifting his head to gain his footing. Henri jerked the reins to pull the horse's head up, growled at the beast again, and dug his heels into the animal's ribs. The bay stumbled forward, head drooping and then he staggered, fell forward on his chest. Henri jumped free as the animal rolled to its side, chest heaving as he fought for breath, then groaned as he breathed his last.

Henri snarled, "Now what'm I gonna do!" He stepped to the downed animal and kicked at its neck, venting his anger and frustration. He stopped, looking around, then with a glance at the tracks that came from the timbered ridges before him, he grabbed at his rifle that was in the scabbard on the underneath side of the horse, but he could not free it. He sat down and put his feet against the back of the horse and the cantle of the saddle and tugged, fighting to pull the rifle from under the carcass, then it gave way and he fell to his back, rifle in hand.

At his belt he had a scabbarded knife and a pistol. His powder horn and possibles pouch hung from his shoulder. He reached for the saddle bags but realized he could not pull them free, so he searched the one side for anything useful, finding only a ragged and stained shirt, some crumbs from jerky and little else. Shaking his head, he stood, looked at the tracks and started toward the timbered ridge. *Don't need nuthin' else. I'll just take what I want from them wimmen, after . . .* and finished his thought with a cackle.

As he neared the trees, he had a faint hint of smoke, but it was the stagnant smell of a doused fire. He paused, trying to see through the trees and seeing nothing, moved into the scattered juniper, wending his way through, carefully watching for movement or sign of a clearing. Within thirty yards, the ponderosa crowded the juniper and cedar and circled a clearing.

Henri stopped, searching the moonlit clearing. He saw two lean-tos, blankets showing at the edges, a fire ring with cold coals, a stack of gear by the trees and four or five horses picketed on the far side. He grinned, knowing he found exactly what he was looking for, the camp with the women.

He started toward the lean-tos, picking his steps and licking his lips, his grin grew wide and his eyes showed white as he neared the edge of the blankets. He reached with the muzzle of his rifle and nudged the sleeping form, "Git outta them blankets, you!" he growled.

The figure kicked at the intruder, sitting up and holding the blanket before her. Henri couldn't see the form and stepped back, "C'mon outta there!" he ordered.

Dove slowly scooted to the edge of the lean-to, lay the blanket to the side and started to rise, looking at the mousy man before her. "Who are you?" she asked, glaring at him.

He started to step back, but a hand covered his mouth and the razor edge of a knife was at his throat. He squirmed, lifting the rifle muzzle and pulled the trigger. The rifle bucked and roared, the smoke shooting the grey cloud into the air beside the lean-to, and Henri tried to squirm away, but the grip was tight, and the knife drew blood. He froze, feeling the blood trickle down his neck, when he heard the voice, "Drop the rifle!"

His eyes flared and he glared at the woman before him, started to swing the muzzle as a club, but the knife dug deep and slit his throat from ear to ear. Blood spurted over his neck and chest, as the hand released its grip and he fell to his knees, trying to draw air but choking on his own blood. As he started to fall to the blankets, Dove kicked him aside and he fell to his face in the dirt. She looked up at Cougar, "Where were you?"

"Bobcat had stirred early," she answered as she wiped the blade on the britches of Henri Petit, then stood, "so I fed him and lay him down. When he dozed, I went to the trees to relieve myself and heard him," nodding at the dead man.

Dove smiled, shook her head, and turned back as she heard Squirrel whimper. Cougar knelt beside the form of Henri to get a handful of dirt to wipe off the blood, then picked up the man's rifle and went to the stack of gear.

***

As Gabe started toward the trees, Wolf veered toward the trail taken by Ezra, but Gabe called him, "Wolf, here, to the trees." But he refused, looking at the trail and the edge of the trees. Gabe shrugged, "Alright, I'm comin'," and gigged Ebony to follow. Ezra had just disappeared around the point of the trees when a rifle shot shattered the darkness. Gabe slapped legs to Ebony and the big black lunged forward to follow Wolf who took off at a run. The stallion bumped the rear of Ezra's bay as they both came to a sudden stop at the edge of the clearing, the pack horse trotting up behind them. Gabe looked at the stack of gear and saw Cougar Woman standing, hands on hips, staring at the two sudden arrivals. Ezra saw Dove stick her head from the lean-to, the clatter of hooves had startled her. Ezra pointed to the dead man and Wolf that was sniffing at the carcass, looked at Gabe and said, "Looks like they already took care of the problem."

Both men shook their heads, slid from their saddles as Ezra asked, "What's for breakfast?"

32 / RETURN

The men dragged the body of the little voyageur away from camp, rolling it into a dry wash and pushing the bank atop the crumpled form. The rising sun had illumined the day but was slow in peeking over the top of the slope behind their camp. Long shadows of juniper and piñon stretched across the dry wash, bending with the ravine's steep sides. Gabe looked heavenward, "Lord, I can't say anything good about that rascal down there, didn't know him well and didn't want to. He was a murderin' back-stabbin' skunk, far as I know, but You knew him better. If you've been holdin' a place for him, well, that's your doin', but I don't believe your Word would allow it. So, I guess all I have to say is, we're glad he's gone. Amen!"

Ezra shook his head as he let a grin spread through his whiskers, then looked up at his friend, "Since when you think you can tell God what to do?"

"I wasn't tellin', just explainin'," offered Gabe. "Sides, I didn't hear you preachin' any great sermon!"

"Not about to, not over that!" he nodded over his shoulder as they walked away from the gulch. The smell of perking coffee and frying pork belly came from the camp and Ezra grinned, "We best hurry, breakfast might get cold!" and started to the camp at a trot. Gabe followed close behind, chuckling all the way. It was the release of tension that added a touch of giddiness to the men's usual banter and he was smiling as he dropped to the ground to accept the offered cup of coffee from a smiling Cougar Woman.

Gabe was seated on the ground, leaning back against a log near the cookfire. Cougar sat beside him on the log, her calf touching his arm as she dropped her hand to his shoulder. He looked up at her as she smiled at him and she asked, "What now?"

He took a sip of coffee, held it with both hands before him as he looked at the low flames licking at the frying pan, "Well, I reckon we'll rest up a day or so, then head back to the cabin." He turned to look up at her again, saw her smile of approval, "Does that mean you like the idea?"

"Yes. I like our cabin. It will be good to be home."

"Yup, I agree. It will be good to be home," replied Gabe, bringing the hot cup to his lips for another long draught.

After a filling breakfast, both men crawled into their blankets in the two lean-tos. They shared the space with the snoozing little ones, but it did not take long for them to fall asleep. It had been most of two days since they slept and their weariness had caught up with them. Dove and Cougar puttered with the clean-up until Cougar suggested they go to the river to replenish their food stores. Dove asked, "What about the little ones?" glancing to the lean-tos.

Cougar Woman smiled, "They will sleep and if they wake, their fathers are near," a mischievous glint showing in her eye as the corner of her mouth lifted.

Dove stifled a giggle, grabbed a parfleche and her rifle and accouterments and followed Cougar as they started to the river. The Bitterroot river twisted its way through the valley no more than six hundred yards below their camp. With an abundance of berry bushes on its bank, the women gathered chokecherries, service berries and some bright red buffalo berries, but passed up the kinnikinnick. Low growing strawberries and raspberries and thimbleberries joined the rest in the parfleche. Dove spotted some tall stalks with wilted blue flowers and knew it to be camas and was soon digging for the roots.

Dove's rifle hung from a sling at her shoulder, but Cougar had brought her bow and the weapon, already strung, hung from the quiver of arrows at her back. While they searched for berries and roots, Cougar constantly watched for any danger or game. She had just stood after gathering a couple hands full of raspberries when movement made her freeze in place. She was sheltered by a cluster of willows, then leaned down to peer through to the animal at the sand bar on the far side of the river. She was surprised to see a small herd of bighorn sheep tiptoeing to the water. These animals usually stay in or near the mountains and were seldom seen in the flats, but she looked at the mountain range that bordered the valley and knew it to be no more than two to three miles away.

Cougar motioned to Dove who was humming as she dug the camas bulbs and motioned to the river. Dove frowned, lifted up and saw the sheep, then looked back at Cougar. She saw the woman nocking an arrow, readying for a shot at one of the sheep. She looked back at the herd, saw what she thought Cougar would take, a young ram, horns not even a half curl that was standing broadside to the woman and watching the lambs run and jump.

Cougar slowly rose, bow at full draw and let the arrow fly. It whispered across the forty yards and buried itself in the low chest of the ram, causing it to jump almost straight up, take two short bounds and fall. The others scampered together, leaving the river at a run and headed directly across the valley toward the mountains.

Cougar saw the arrow hit its mark and watched as

the ram fell. On its side, it kicked twice, then lay still. She looked at Dove, "Now I've got to wade the river to bring it back!"

Dove shrugged, "You could have asked it to come closer before you shot it!" laughing. The water was less than waist deep on Cougar as she waded across and stood, tunic, leggings and moccasins soaking wet, over the downed animal. In short order she had field dressed the ram and lifted it to her shoulders to wade back across the river.

While Cougar was busy field dressing the ram, Dove cut a long cottonwood sapling and had it ready when Cougar came from the water. The women bound the legs together over the sapling, then with the carcass hanging between them, the sapling on their shoulders, they started back to camp.

All was quiet when they returned and they dropped their cargo and began fashioning some drying racks from the gathered willows. By the time the men and the little ones aroused, the sheep had been skinned, the smoke racks readied and strips of meat were hanging over the low burning alder coals with smoke curing the fresh cuts.

Chipmunk was the first to toddle out of the lean-to, rubbing his eyes as he staggered toward his mother. She smiled, arms outstretched and scooped him up as he came near. She hugged him tight, then took him to the edge of the clearing to tend to business. A whimper came from the lean-to with Gabe. Cougar smiled but waited to see what Gabe would do with the little one. But within a quick moment, the little one quieted and nothing stirred. Cougar's curiosity got the better of her and she tiptoed near to peek into the shadows. Gabe was on his back, Bobcat on his belly and both Gabe's arms were folded over the boy, keeping him secure as both had drifted back to sleep. She smiled and walked back to the fire for a cup of coffee.

By the time the men aroused, the women had loin steaks sizzling and broiling over the fire, biscuits baking under some coals in the dutch oven, camas bulbs buried in the coals and a pot of mixed berries fermenting in a pot with a handful of sugar. The men rose to the aroma of the cooking and rolled from the blankets, each holding the babies as they came from the lean-tos, but they were quick to hand them off as they began whimpering and reaching for their mothers. Gabe grabbed for a cup and the coffee pot, pouring Ezra's cup full then his own and sat down on the log to watch as the women fed the babies.

Ezra looked at Gabe, "So, what'chu reckon it is? June, July, later?"

Gabe looked at his friend, thought about the question and frowned, remembering what all had taken place since they left the cabin in the early spring, but early spring in the mountains is closer to summer in the lowlands. "Late June, maybe July. Not August yet."

Ezra pondered on it a moment, "Yeah, mebbe so," then sipped some more coffee.

Gabe asked, "Why? Got somewhere you need to be?"

Ezra grinned, "Nope," then nodded to the women and little ones, "already there!"

***

Each one trailed a packhorse, while Gabe let the big grey they gained from Northwest, trail along at his own pace. He had become used to traveling without a lead and staying close to Ebony and occasionally crowded the steeldust that usually followed the big stallion. They had re-distributed the packs and none were heavy loaded, yet Gabe set an easy pace as they began their return trip to the cabin. Cougar asked, "How long will it take?"

"Oh, four, five days, maybe a week. Depends," he smiled at his woman. "Getting anxious to be home?"

"A little. It will be good to be home and let Bobcat play. Dove wants Chipmunk to have a place to run, he is walking so well, but he gets in a hurry and falls down," she laughed at the thought, smiling. "Our boy will soon be walking also."

"Already?" asked Gabe, frowning. She smiled at his response, nodding her head.

33 / HOME

They followed the Bitterroot upstream through the wide valley, passing the scene of the skirmish between the Northwest company and the Hudson Bay band, early on the second day. Gabe glanced to Ezra, "Reckon they did as they said, went south and east from here, headin' to Crow country."

"Thompson said he'd traded with 'em before, the Blackfoot too, so, reckon they'll do alright. What with the plunder from the Hudson Bay bunch, they'll have 'em a profitable trip!" responded Ezra.

"I'm just glad it's all behind us. Bad enough when we gotta fight the natives, but when your own kind turn against you . . ."

"Own kind? They weren't my kind! Don't lump me in with them brigands!" declared an indignant Ezra.

Gabe chuckled, "Alright, alright, the sooner we forget about 'em the better!" But he knew, as always, there would be no forgetting. Times when there is bloodletting and killing are always branded into the memory, never to be erased, seldom dispelled and too often haunting.

It was nearing the end of the second day when Cougar saw familiar country, looked to the mountains and recognized a canyon, and pointed to their right, "Is not that the trail we traveled to go to the Nez Percé?"

Gabe smiled and answered, "Sure is! Remember that little lake that lies in the mouth of that canyon?"

Cougar looked at Gabe, smiling, "Yes! I remember that! It was beautiful!"

"Yes it was and probably still is. We're in familiar country now. The trail we came up on is in that cut between those hills," he was pointing to the south and the mountains that crowded the end of the valley.

"So, we're three, four days from home?" she asked, her head cocked to the side as she looked at her man. She glanced down to the cradleboard that held Bobcat and hung beside her left leg, then reached down to reassure the little one.

"Bout that," answered Gabe. He pointed to a bend in the river that held a grassy meadow and some mature cottonwoods, "How 'bout we make camp there?"

***

Another day traveling south along the Bitterroot River took them into the mountains and when the Bitterroot bent to the east, they pointed south, but not before Ezra provided some fresh brook trout for their supper. Late morning of the following day, they left the southbound trail and turned on the usual path due east, bound for the familiar village of their friends, the Salish.

It was a narrow valley nestled between black timber covered hills that held the trail they chose. It was a pleasant change after the barren hills that shouldered the east edge of the Bitterroot valley, the hills often called the badlands. But it was pleasant because this was familiar country, a land with both bitter and pleasing memories, but their minds were full of good thoughts and remembrances as they drew ever closer to the land they knew so well.

They came from the headwaters of the creek known only as Trail Creek because of the oft-used trail in the valley and followed the twisting stream through that valley, the trail shouldering the hills on the north side. The sun was at their back and the shadows were stretching long beside them when they broke into the open and saw the horse herd of the Salish village of Plenty Bears and his people. They were immediately spotted by the young men that stood watch over the herd and had gone but a short distance before two of the young men rode up to stop them.

When they neared, they were instantly recognized as the two sons of Spotted Eagle, Red Hawk and White Feather. When the young men recognized them, there were smiles and greetings all around and the two turned to ride beside the returning friends. Red Hawk asked, "So, did Two Drums and Little Owl join?"

Cougar Woman smiled, nodding, "Yes, they did. It is a good village where they will live. Two Drums mother and her sister welcomed both of them and they will be close."

Red Hawk dropped his eyes, then looked back to Cougar, "Will she be allowed to teach?"

"Yes, they were happy that she would share what she has learned. Two Drums will also teach the young people with her."

Red Hawk smiled, glancing at White Feather, "That is good. We," motioning to White Feather and himself, "have been able to tell many the things we learned about God and the Bible and more."

Gabe glanced at Ezra, both men smiling broadly, and said, "We are proud of you Red Hawk," then to his brother, "And you too, White Feather."

Red Hawk said, "I see you have the appaloosa with you and she is big with colt."

"That's right, have any of the others dropped yet?" asked Gabe, referring to the three mares bred by Ebony as part of an agreement between him and Red

Hawk's father, Spotted Eagle.

"My father says it could be any day, but I think it will be longer," answered the young man.

White Feather had kicked his horse to a canter, rushing to be the first to tell the village of the return of their friends. When the others rode into the village, there were many that had come near to welcome them, waving, shouting greetings, reaching up to touch them and some of the youngsters greeted Wolf with a touch or even a hug. He was a familiar figure in the village and Wolf remembered the people as well.

As they neared the central compound of the village, they saw the stoic Plenty Bears, his wife Grasshopper, Spotted Eagle and an unfamiliar woman beside him, waiting to greet the returning friends. Gabe and the others lifted their hands in greeting and at the motion of Plenty Bears, they slid to the ground, several others coming near to hug the women and greet the men. Gabe turned to the chief and extended his hand as the chief came close, but instead of shaking hands, they clasped forearms to greet each other. A similar greeting was given by Spotted Eagle, then he turned to the woman beside him, and said to Gabe, "This is my woman, Prairie Flower." She nodded and Gabe said, "Good to meet you Prairie Flower." Then turning to his woman, Gabe continued, "This is my wife, Cougar Woman, my friend Black Buffalo and his wife, Grey Dove."

***

They spent the night with the Salish, enjoying the time of remembering and telling about the events of the summer. Prairie Flower had been the wife of a friend who was killed in the Blackfoot attack and the two had found solace and comfort with one another. It was a natural union and both seemed to be happy. Gabe turned to Red Hawk and asked, "So, are you ready for your try at horse training?"

The young man grinned, squirming a little and answered, "I have been working with some yearlings in the herd, it has been good. But I am anxious for the colts to come for I will start with them right away!"

"Right away? Not even gonna let them grow a little?" asked Ezra.

"No, I will start with them right away. I believe there is a special time to make that connection, that bond, that will make it easier to train the colts and yearlings as they grow. They become my friends and we understand each other." He was enthusiastic in his explanation, but did not look directly at his father and Gabe detected there was some disagreement between the two, but he let it lie and did not broach the subject.

"Well, it will be interesting to see how you do. Perhaps I can learn a thing or two from you!" declared Gabe.

The rest of the evening was an enjoyable one,

everyone sharing and suggesting future times that should be shared together. Before they turned in for the night, it was agreed that word would be sent to the cabin whenever the colts came and that everyone would return, once they were all on the ground. They departed the village before first light, leaving their friends undisturbed, knowing the day's travel would be long and tiring.

***

The sun was almost blinding as it settled in the cut between the western mountains. The group had turned from the broad valley trail to the narrow and less used trail that bent to the west into their valley. Ebony had recognized the country and quickened his pace and the others were not to be left behind. The trail twisted and turned through the black timber, broke into the open in the lower meadow, then climbed the shoulder into the aspen and spruce, leaving the little lake in the valley bottom. When the trail bent back on itself, they moved through the last stretch of timber into the clearing that held the cabin.

Gabe stopped, Cougar and the others came alongside, and they looked at the cabin. Grass had grown tall in the clearing and beside and behind the cabin, but the building stood strong and firm. Gabe nudged Ebony forward, but did not stop in front of the struc-

ture and rode to the left side to look at the side and the
rear where the cabin butted up to the cliff face. Only
then did he relax, for that was where the grizzly had
once before, ripped the wall and back to get into the
cavern behind the cabin, but everything was secure
and sound. He laughed at himself as he stepped down,
then lifted the cradleboard with Bobcat off the saddle
to hand to Cougar Woman.

"We'll take care of the animals while you ladies
make yourself to home! But, be careful when you
open the door, there could be varmints!"

Cougar slipped Gabe's pistol from his belt, grinned
at him and said, "For varmints! Be sure to knock before *you* come in!"

They stripped the packs to put them on the porch,
led the horses to the corral at the back and stripped
the saddles and tack. After brushing them all down,
they were released into the pasture and the men
watched as they rolled and went to the water. Gabe
looked at Ezra, "Good to be home!"

"Yup. And I'm hungry!" declared Ezra as the men
started back to the cabin.

***

The meal over, the basics unpacked and put away,
Gabe pushed the other packs aside and brought
chairs onto the porch. With each one holding a cup

of steaming coffee, they sat and enjoyed the cool of the evening, bright stars and a full moon hanging overhead. Words were not necessary for when good friends are together their presence says all that needs to be said, the only sound heard was the sipping of coffee, the creak of the rocking chair and the cicadas in the woods, the coyotes in the flats and the wise old owl that asked the only question. Wolf lifted his head as if to answer the question, glanced at the others, then dropped his contented head between his paws and closed his eyes. It was good to be home.

WATCH FOR: PAITUE PASSAGE (STONECROFT SAGA 11)

When the Salish War Leader, Spotted Eagle appeared in the clearing before their cabin, Gabe and Ezra weren't sure what to think. This man had shown himself to be their friend, and now he invited them to join him and the village on a buffalo hunt. With winter just around the corner, it seemed the likely thing to do, but had they known what the journey would bring, they might have had second thoughts.

Their discovery of the massacre of the Paiute village and the three survivors that told the story, was just the beginning of the fight against the warring Waiilatpus. A pursuit across the lava beds of the Snake River plains, a fight in the dead of night, a thundering stampede of buffalo, and a horde of bugs that shrouded the entire valley were just the added complications to a simple buffalo hunt, or perhaps more, and blood would be spilt, lives changed, and decisions made.

AVAILABLE NOVEMBER 2020

ABOUT THE AUTHOR

Born and raised in Colorado into a family of ranchers and cowboys, B.N. Rundell is the youngest of seven sons. Juggling bull riding, skiing, and high school, graduation was a launching pad for a hitch in the Army Paratroopers. After the army, he finished his college education in Springfield, MO, and together with his wife and growing family, entered the ministry as a Baptist preacher.

Together, B.N. and Dawn raised four girls that are now married and have made them proud grandparents. With many years as a successful pastor and educator, he retired from the ministry and followed in the footsteps of his entrepreneurial father and started a successful insurance agency, which is now in the hands of his trusted nephew. He has also been a successful audiobook narrator and has recorded many books for several award-winning authors. Now finally realizing his life-long dream, B.N. has turned his efforts to writing a variety of books, from children's picture books and young adult adventure books, to the historical fiction and western genres.

Made in the USA
Monee, IL
30 July 2021

74574581R10162